To Adelle

The Hearts of Elephants and Men

And other stories of Africa

Best wishes

MARTIN GWENT LEWIS

JAN 2004

Lifestyles Press, Inc
P.O. Box 493
Greensboro, NC 27455
1-888-742-2155

Introduction

I arrived at Entebbe Airport in Uganda as the sun rose over Lake Victoria one November day in 1965. I had no idea what to expect or what my life would be like during the ensuing three years.

My position was entitled "Lecturer in Geographical Pathology," University of East Africa. My knowledge of pathology was minimal and geography so rudimentary that I had to consult an atlas to see where my future home was in that vast continent.

To my surprise, waiting for us at the airport at that early hour was a remarkable man, the Professor of Pathology at the medical school in Kampala. It was not customary for Senior Professors to meet junior lecturers at the crack of dawn and help carry their suitcases. Professor Michael Hutt not only became my mentor but to this day has remained my dear friend. He inspired me and my colleagues and taught us a great deal about tropical pathology, Africa and Africans.

His predecessor, Professor J.N.P. Davies, who also remains a close and dear friend had previously developed a department there and Professor Hutt built on it in a magnificent way.

Between November, 1965 and November, 1968 Uganda became my home and it still has a very special place in my heart. The people I worked with came from a variety of backgrounds and countries but we all had one thing in common. Inspired by our leaders, we had an intimate relationship and a growing concern of Africa.

With the exception of "The Shoeshine Boy of Addis Ababa" the other short stories are based on personal experiences. Most of the characters were real people – some of them are still alive – their names, however, have been altered.

They were difficult times in Uganda in the 1960's as the country went through the transition period from being a British protectorate to being an independent and at first, however short, a democratic state. Despite the terrible years of the reign of Idi Amin, the resilient people of Uganda have survived.

I would like to dedicate these short stories to them and to the numerous colleagues who helped me have an appreciation of Africa and Africans, particularly Professor J.N.P. Davies and Professor Michael Hutt.

Table of Contents

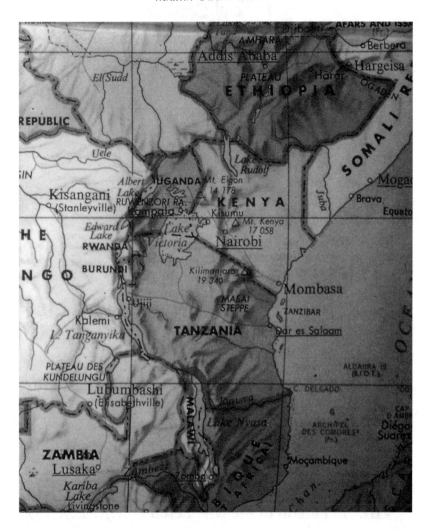

East Africa

THE HEARTS

OF ELEPHANTS

AND MEN

"What on earth is that?" Richard asked, as he sank to his knees before the long plastic bag which had been rolled across the floor of his office by a young man who had the air of a Persian carpet merchant, rather than the veterinary pathologist he claimed to be.

"Don't you recognize the aorta, Dr. Jones?"

"Yes. I suppose I do," Richard said. "It's certainly familiar, but it's so damned big."

"Well, of course it is...it's from an elephant. I'll bet you've never seen one before, have you?"

"You're damned right I haven't," Richard said, as he knelt closer to examine the specimen in more detail.

"Well, it sure looks like a large version of the human aorta, but this one shows evidence of arteriosclerosis. Look at those calcified areas," Richard said, as much to himself as to his companion.

1

"Exactly!" shouted the young man excitedly, clapping his hands with delight.

Richard looked up at him and suppressed a smile.

Kevin McCrorey was a veterinarian who was more interested in pathology than clinical practice, and had recently been awarded a scholarship from the Royal Society. Instead of spending the money carefully on some insignificant research in England, to everyone's horror, he spent most of the grant on a Land Rover. He drove across Europe to North Africa, and finally down though the Sudan into Kenya, and ended up in Kampala in Uganda.

Richard was about to ask why he had been singled out for this privilege of the young vet's visit when the door opened and in came the head of the department. He was a man who was highly regarded by his staff, and had authority, not from a sense of power, but because the staff had great respect for him. It had often been said that any one of them would have attempted to assassinate Idi Armin if he'd simply mentioned it.

Within a few minutes the professor made arrangements for Richard to be a Ph.D. supervisor. He was to help young Kevin McCrorey to obtain this degree from the University of Cambridge. Richard's responsibility was to make sure that McCrorey did.

It was not that it did not have the potential for being an interesting study, particularly since the circumstances were unique indeed, but Richard had planned some research projects that were closer to his heart over the next few months, and this would certainly be a problem. Trying to ease his way out of the situation, he suggested to McCrorey that specimens would be brought to the lab, and there

Richard would help him with the pathology.

The amazing thing about the proposed project was that it had all sorts of official authorization and approval. For a man who had demonstrated such entrepreneurism as this young veterinarian, it seemed amazing to Richard the McCrorey had managed to persuade so many people to support what, at first sight, sounded like a crazy idea: the study of arteriosclerosis in the wild African elephant. As McCrorey had already pointed out, there was only one case of arteriosclerosis observed in an elephant, and that was in an old beast that had died in the Munich Zoo some twenty years previously.

The situation was timely, however. That year in the famous Murchison Game Park, in northern Uganda, there was a serious over-population of elephants. It had been planned to crop large numbers of these animals. At this moment appears McCrorey, as if the project had been designed with him in mind.

Richard could hardly argue his way out of the circumstances; they were in every sense of the word unbelievably unique.

"I still can't understand," Richard said later that afternoon as they were discussing the details, "why you can't just send the hearts down here from the game park when they've shot the animals, and I'll deal with the pathology for you."

"You don't understand, Dr. Jones."

"Oh, for goodness sake, don't call me Dr. Jones. Call me Richard," he insisted.

"Well, Richard, it's like this. Have you any idea how big an elephant's heart is?"

"No, I suppose I don't," Richard sighed.

3

"Well, it would fill that large old armchair you have over there in the corner of the office. How many of those do you think I could fit into a Land Rover and send down three hundred miles?"

Richard admitted, reluctantly, that McCrorey had made a decisive point. It did not take very long for the axe to completely fall on Richard's projected plans when the professor completed all the necessary arrangements for Richard to accompany McCrorey on a field expedition to join the cropping expedition in the game park.

The dirt road on which they were traveling was well known to Richard. He sat in the Land Rover dozing in the afternoon heat and thought of other, more pleasant times when he had traveled the same road on various fishing expeditions in the earlier months after his arrival in Uganda. He idly watched the small African farms and villages which occasionally could be glimpsed through the trees at the side of the road, when quite suddenly and abruptly there was a sharp sound like a rifle being discharged, followed immediately by a sensation of swaying and sinuous movement of the vehicle. Richard immediately recognized this as a burst tire.

He had to admit that McCrorey handled the situation very well, and brought the Land Rover to a reasonably safe halt, perched slightly over the edge of the ditch at the side of the road, but thankfully not in it. Burst tires were certainly a well-known accompaniment to journeys on the roads in East Africa, but to Richard's horror, when he examined the spare tire which was to replace the damaged one, it was almost as smooth as the surface of his desk at home.

4

"How on earth could you bring a spare tire as bad as this one -- a man who's traveled as much as you claim to have done?" Richard shouted at him.

"Oh, well. I forgot," said McCrorey with a shrug.

"You forgot! Oh, hell! All right, there's no point in putting that spare on. It won't last very long at all. Let's get some hot patches out and we'll repair the one that's already on there." This was an old technique that Richard had picked up from seasoned travelers in East Africa.

McCrorey looked sheepishly at Richard and tried to give one of his charming smiles, and explained that somehow he had forgotten to bring the hot patches and the tire repair kit.

Richard was so furious that he could not express himself at all, and sat down, feeling almost like crying. There was no option but to put the spare tire on, and the torn burst one in the back of the Land Rover.

McCrorey then proceeded to demonstrate more of his idiosyncratic behavior. He began to drive faster and faster. Richard leaned across and trying very politely, said, "You do realize, of course, that the tire we have on there is like an eggshell, and could rupture at any moment. Why on earth are you going as fast as this?"

"Oh, well, it's obvious isn't it, old chap? I mean, the sooner we get to the next place and get the tire fixed, the better."

Richard sat back exasperated. Within a few seconds there was another bang and a lurch, and this time the vehicle was very difficult to control because of the speed, and indeed they ended up this time partly in the ditch, with luckily the offending wheel sticking out into the air. There was no point in him saying "I told you so," and he resisted the temptation

5

to do so.

Now what do we do Richard thought. Well, there was nothing to do. Two burst tires, no way of repairing them, so they sat down at the side of the road, neither speaking, both afraid to for different reasons.

Richard tried to assess the situation and took out the map, estimating that they were fifty miles from Chobee Lodge, which was their destination for that night, and the next town beyond that was a hundred miles further. He couldn't remember whether there was, in fact, a village or a town a shorter distance that they'd already passed, but had a vague feeling that there was one perhaps ten or fifteen miles back. It was all rather theoretical since there was no way of getting to either of them at that point.

While he was pondering this situation, a cloud of red dust appeared on the horizon, over a hill to the north of them.

"Let's hope they're sympathetic enough to stop," McCrorey said.

Richard didn't answer.

The car was a small Fiat, and it came to a rapid halt as the driver saw the two men at the side of the road. Out of the driving seat jumped a small excited man with a balding head, wearing a nondescript khaki bush jacket and shorts. He rushed across and greeted the two men in a thick Italian accent.

"Ricardo, my friend! What do you do here in the middle of nowhere?'

Richard recognized his old friend, Paolo Corti, a surgeon at the Mission Hospital in Gulu, a remarkable little Italian full of life, and a delight to see, particularly under those adverse circumstances.

Richard explained the situation with a certain amount of embarrassment.

"I will take the wheel down the road," Corti said, waving his hands in the air. "Unfortunately, no room for people, you see," and he pointed. There were two portly nuns jammed into the back of the Fiat, who obviously had decided not to exert the necessary energy to get out of the car at this point.

"There is a bus following us a few miles behind," Corti said. "Your friend must travel on the bus and meet us at the garage down the road and then hopefully find a way back." Paolo was quite apologetic. "You see, of course, my friend, I would do this willingly and come back too, but the ladies...well, you understand."

Richard nodded and Corti slapped him warmly on the back.

"You must remember to come back when the grass is low, and we go elephant shooting."

Richard smiled. He was about to go elephant shooting, but that would have been quite a different experience with Dr. Corti, he was sure. Richard was going to explain to him why they were going to the game park, but decided that it might get the Italian so excited that he'd insist on joining them, and then he had no idea how he would explain it the authorities.

Paolo Corti was a marvelous surgeon and a wonderful missionary, but he had an unbelievably powerful urge to kill elephants. He was restricted in this respect by the game laws of Uganda, which at that time, before the rise of Idi Armin, was still fairly well controlled. Richard thought about it afterward, as the prospect of seeing the Italian's eyes as he explained to him that they were apparently going to be

7

shooting some 2000 elephants to keep the numbers down.

Sure enough, some thirty minutes later, a typical African bus came to a halt in a cloud of dust opposite the Land Rover. Despite the fact that the vehicle seemed to be more than filled to capacity, McCrorey managed to get in. Even the roof, as usual, was piled with boxes, including cages containing chickens. As the bus disappeared into the distance, Richard settled down in the shade of a nearby tree and began to read the paperback he'd brought with him for such possible occasion. He had read it before, more than once, but Jerome K. Jerome's classic book, "Three Men in a Boat," always seemed new, and there was always something in that story that made him laugh.

Richard suddenly looked up and there were five children standing and staring at him.

"Jambo," he addressed them.

Instead of the customary reply in Swahili, the oldest child, a boy of about twelve, bowed respectfully, and said in English, "Good afternoon, sir. Is that a reading book you are reading?"

Richard admitted that it was, and the boy glanced around to his young companions.

"Would you kindly read it for us, sir? The children would like that."

Before Richard could answer, the group settled in a semicircle around him and looked at him expectantly. He shrugged his shoulders and started to read. The young boy acted as an interpreter, and sentence by sentence translated the story of an Edwardian boating holiday on the Thames.

Considering these African children had probably never been more than twenty miles from the small village, they were a very devoted audience. At one point Richard laughed out loud at one passage that always seemed to amuse him, and noticed that the children's faces remained blank. He realized that the young boy's translation could hardly give credit to the understated humor of Jerome, which was so English that possibly even Americans would find it less than amusing.

Amazingly, over an hour slipped by very quickly, when without any warning the leader of the group stood up and signaled to the others that it was time to leave. He thanked Richard profusely, but his eyes were drawn longingly to the book. Richard couldn't resist it. He handed him the small literary treasure and the boy's eyes opened wide with gratitude. Once again, bowing courteously, he also slid away into the bush.

McCrorey eventually arrived in a Peugeot 404 taxi, jammed with passengers, the roof covered with bicycles, and the repaired tire.

"How did you pass the time?" he casually asked as they drove toward Chobee Lodge.

"Oh, I read a little," Richard said, and he wondered to himself how the young boy would enjoy reading "Three Men in a Boat."

Richard loved his creature comforts, and the prospect of staying at the beautiful African anomaly of a luxurious hotel in the middle of a game park had a strong appeal. Chobee Safari Lodge was a well laid out series of buildings, with a main dining room and numerous smaller extensions with cozy individual living quarters. One of its most spectacular features was a verandah facing the steep incline to the rushing waters of the Uganda White Nile. The surrounding low scrub land and the savannah was rich with game.

Having spent several hours cramped in the Land Rover, Richard longed to stay at the lodge that night. He could picture himself sitting there on that verandah with a cool beer, stretching his legs, looking at the game coming down to the river, and with the prospect of an excellent meal and comfortable bed to sleep in. This was not to be.

McCrorey suddenly became authoritative and persistent. He insisted that the hunters in their camp were waiting for them, and they had promised to be there that night. Even the manager of the hotel, who of course was on Richard's side, tried to persuade them that there was barely an hour left of daylight, and that traveling through that particular area of the game park in the dark was filled with dangers. McCrorey would not budge, and so with instructions from the manager of how to get to the main base camp, they set off. Richard was not in a particularly good mood.

In the rapidly developing African dusk, they traveled through areas of the game reserve rarely visited by tourists. The road was rough and difficult to follow, at times reverting to only a track. They passed closely by elephants, gazelles, and warthogs, and several lions lying at the side of the road. At one point they were even pursued for a few hundred yards by a pair of rhinos. The sun set rapidly indeed, and they continued slowly through the ever-narrowing track by the light of the headlamps.

This man will be the death of me, Richard thought. In his year in East Africa this was the first time that he'd broken the rule of never traveling by night, and particularly in the bush.

"For goodness sake, slow down, Kevin!" Richard said irritably, as they barely missed the trunk of a large baobab tree.

Then, abruptly, through the trees, they saw the lights. Richard didn't really know what to expect, but it was certainly no Boy Scout gathering. It resembled more of a military encampment. There were several large tents with tables, and many smaller tents apart from the others. There appeared to be a great bustle of activity. They had obviously arrived just in time for dinner.

The warm welcome awaiting them certainly made Richard feel better, and within a few minutes they were introduced to the various members of the hunting team. The man in charge was John Phillips, and with him was his wife, Sylvia. What amazed Richard even more was that they had with them an eight-week-old baby.

Phillips was not exactly what Richard imagined a professional big game hunter would be like. He was a small, thin man with baggy khaki shorts which seemed to make his legs look like sticks. They were provided with sundowners, and sat at a large table under the stars. After his second gin and tonic, Richard began to feel less of a longing for the comfort of the game lodge.

"I've never been big game hunting before," Richard said to his host.

There were looks of amusement on the faces of the others around the table. Sylvia Phillips smiled indulgently and walked away to one of the tents.

"Dr. Jones, let me put you right on a few things." Phillips leaned back in his canvas chair. "We're not big game hunters. As far as I'm concerned, anyone who kills animals for the sheer fun of doing it is beneath my contempt."

Richard was puzzled, and said, "Why do you do this

11

particular job then, if you don't mind my asking?"

"Well, it's what I know how to do best," Phillips replied. "If the animals have to be controlled, it's better that a professional should do it. I at least know how to do it humanely and we don't do this for fun. What chance, after all, has an animal got against men with high-powered rifles and telescopic lenses?"

"What about these stories one hears of hunters being injured or killed?"

"The only ones that that happens to are usually the incompetent. I'll show you what I mean tomorrow when we actually go after the elephants. Don't get me wrong, some of my best friends and close colleagues make their living taking rich Americans and Germans out to shoot animals for the sport. I don't think many of them really enjoy it; it's a job, and since some of us were born out here in Africa we have become used to certain lifestyles, if you know what I mean. I regard myself as being a fortunate one in that I specialize in this kind of cropping of animals in game parks where controlling the numbers is an essential part of management."

The conversation was interrupted by the arrived of Africans at the table with plates of food. It was a wonderful feeling to sit under the stars and eat a hearty meal with such companions, and Richard stared at his plate, which contained the largest steak he'd ever seen.

"This is marvelous meat. How do you manage to get it?" Richard asked without thinking. "In Kampala all we can manage is a scrawny-looking beefsteak from cattle that almost died on their way to the market."

There were grins and suppressed laughter around the table. Sylvia gently pointed out that they were surrounded by

12

an unlimited source of meat.

"Of course," Richard said, embarrassedly. "Which particular source are we eating right now?"

"Hippo. Do you like it?"

Richard admitted that he certainly did. He had not expected hippopotamus to either look like or taste like the best rump steak. Somehow he had always associated the animal with the pig family and expected it to look and taste like pork. One of the young zoologists present pointed out that the hippopotamus was more related to the horse than it was to the porcine family. It was his only contribution to the conversation, and he slunk back into his quiet oblivion in the shadows of the tent.

In the cool of the early morning, the small Cessna two-seater bounced across the grass and lifted into the air with apparent ease. Richard glanced across at Phillips, whom he realized was an experienced pilot.

"Look down there, Richard. Isn't that a wonderful sight?" he asked.

They were flying low over country somewhere between the Nile and an area called Elephant Sanctuary. Richard had never been in a small aircraft before, and although he felt a little nervous, his anxiety was swept away by the sheer exuberance of the occasion. There they were flying over the backs of herds of game, and contour hopping over this wilderness, which very few people would be able to see by any other means.

Richard began to feel sorry for Kevin McCrorey, who would have to accompany the rest of the hunting team in a much less comfortable truck as they bounced their way through virtually roadless territory.

"Well, it'll serve him right," he said to himself. "Maybe it'll teach him to get more organized in the future."

He realized, however, that despite the idiosyncrasies, he actually was getting to like young McCrorey, and his ability to take criticism was certainly unbelievable.

They were flying from the base camp to their main advanced hunting camp in the middle of the game park, an area that no tourist groups ever reached. Richard's anxiety came back when they began to circle over the hunting camp, and he saw the runway, if it could be graced with such a name. It was only a rough cleared area in the bush.

He was not particularly further encouraged when Phillips mumbled, "I hope the bastards have cleared all the tree stumps this time. We nearly lost the plane a few weeks ago." Despite this, he landed the small Cessna with consummate skill, and they were soon surrounded by a group of smiling Africans and Phillips' Kenyan partner.

While they waited for the rest of the party to slowly lumber their way through the bush, Richard had the great opportunity to talk to both Phillips and to another one of the zoologists who was already at the advanced camp. It seemed that they would need to remove about 2000 elephants to maintain the balance in that area. This was really astounding to Richard, but when it was explained how destructive these large animals were, and that all the other species were therefore endangered as well, he began to understand.

It seems that the elephants over the centuries have probably created many of the great deserts of the world. One of their unfortunate habits was that they loved to strip the bark off young trees, which subsequently died and led to erosion, and the devastating consequences. Since the animal has virtually no natural enemy, apart from man, and hunting is forbidden within the game parks, they created in a sense their own problem, and over-population was a real problem. But that was in the 1960s, before the wholesale slaughter of these animals solved the problem entirely.

Rival groups of elephants compete for food and grazing territory. They move about in close-knit families consisting of cows and calves, led by an old female. The males are only allowed to join them in the mating season, and are then driven off to live lonely, and what appears to be miserable lives. Anyone who has encountered a lone bull elephant will be aware of the bad mood that so often characterizes these animals. The family groups ranged from ten, up to more than fifty members. and some areas seemed to contain hundreds of them.

Richard was about to ask why they would kill off whole family groups rather than shoot just the old elephants, when it was clearly explained to him that this would simply disrupt the balance and cause even further problems. By taking out entire groups, they did not alter the balance of the existing groups, and hence, hoped that this would solve the problem.

Phillips then explained that it was essential to observe the animals carefully before they started indiscriminate shooting. "Once again," he said, "we're not big game hunters." The most important thing was to identify the old matriarchal leader, and once she was killed, the others would remain in the area with no indication of leadership.

Richard's first encounter with this procedure made him terribly sad indeed. They were driving down the road, out of the hunting camp, when a lone, old elephant lumbered slowly across the pathway in front of them.

"It's unusual to see an old female on her own," Phillips said. "She must be sick and somehow got separated from the rest of the heard. This one we'll take care of, and I'll show you now, doctor, what I mean about big game hunting."

The animal stood there unable to make out what was going on. The approaching hunters were downwind and quiet. Phillips motioned Richard to join him closely, and whispered, "Now you'll see how difficult it is to kill one of these animals."

The elephant was broadside on. Phillips lifted his .275 caliber rifle, aimed and fired. The great animal jerked, fell onto her knees, remained for a few moments as if puzzled by the events, and then slumped down and rolled onto her side in a cloud of dust. There was no drama, no agonizing cry, just a quiet and sad death.

"Would you like to shoot the next one, doctor?" Phillips asked.

"No thanks. You've made your point," Richard replied.

An elephant lying on its side, closeup, is an enormous bulk. Richard had certainly not realized how huge these animals were. The elephant was lying on the slope of a small hill, and Richard approached from below. Some of the African hunters ran forward with their large knives, and one cried out, "Shall we open her up for you, doctor?"

"Sure, go ahead," Richard said.

With great skill, the abdomen was opened so quickly that Richard was taken completely by surprise. He was met halfway up the slope by several hundred yards of intestines, and fell into a messy, moist heap of guts as the entire group roared with laughter. He finally managed to extricate himself and looked bloody and horrible, but saw the scene and joined in the laughter.

He was now one of the camp and part of its fellowship. The dissection of the heart and great vessels also took longer than he had anticipated, and it was only then that he realized that sending the hearts and great vessels to Kampala was virtually impossible. Small samples would have to be taken from the coronary arteries and from the aortas, and shipped down in fixative. He looked at the size of the heart and realized that McCrorey had won his argument.

A group of elephants was identified, and careful observation identified the old cow in charge of the herd. Phillips with his usual skill brought the animal down with his first shot. Instead of the other elephants running off in confusion and panic in all directions, they simply walked around and around their leader, some of them trying to lift her up with their tusks. This gave the other hunters with Phillips the opportunity to pick them off one at a time until the entire group was dead. It was indeed a sad and pathetic sight to see the plain strewn with the carcasses of these large animals.

Richard and McCrorey worked hard, and stripped to their shorts and covered with blood and gore, they obtained their specimens. At least one of the great beasts was identified as being pregnant, and they were able to even sample a fetus inside the uterus. The elephants were aged by their teeth, to some extent more accurately than some of the local Africans. Nothing was wasted. The meat, the skin, and the tusks were separated, and very little was left at the end of the procedure for the army of marabou storks, vultures and hyenas that had encircled the scene. By the following day, there was hardly a

17

trace of a remaining carcass.

That night at the camp there was an air of festivity. Richard and McCrorey, exhausted from their heavy work during the day, strolled through the camp as they watched the Africans laughing and singing around their fires. Richard noticed that they were cooking large chunks of meat on sticks over the open flames. When one of these was offered to Richard as he passed by, he noticed that, in fact, it was the trunk of the elephant cut up into cutlets with a stick going through the nostrils. He had a good sense of adventure and would eat almost anything, but at this he drew the line and made some polite refusals, which caused the Africans to laugh rather than be offended.

The return journey to Kampala was, in many respects, no better than the outgoing trip. This time the burst tires were replaced by spares that Richard had insisted they borrow from Phillips and his colleagues, although this time McCrorey had remembered to obtain repair kits in addition. He had, however, forgotten one vital commodity.

"What do you mean you forgot to bring water, you damned idiot!" Richard yelled at him. "I mean, that's worse than not bringing spare tires or having enough gas, for instance."

For what seemed like an age, neither man spoke.

Richard could not only not bring himself to engage in polite conversation, but his throat was so parched, having worked the morning in the fields over the dead elephants, and now stuck in the dusty Land Rover for several hours, that he could barely move his tongue, and the back of his throat felt like sawdust. All he could think of was an ice-cold beer when they reached Massindi, the first town on the main road to Kampala.

As they drew toward the town, Richard's mood improved, but as they drove into the courtyard of the hotel, he saw, to his horror, one of the attendants pulling the shutters down on what he knew to be the only bar in town. The two men literally leapt out of the Land Rover and, with stiff legs, ran as fast as they could toward the unfortunate hotel servant. He must have realized that his life might be in danger, and immediately opened the shutters and smilingly said, "Would you like beer -- sirs?"

Many years later, the now retired professor, Richard Jones, found himself in a mood for reminiscing. He idly thumbed through his old pile of papers, those past glories long forgotten by contemporary medical science. His eyes lit upon a small reprint, yellow with age, from the Lancet, entitled, "A Study of Arteriosclerosis in the Wild African Elephant." It brought back memories. There had been months of hard labor following that initial safari to the hunting camp, and many specimens laboriously examined microscopically. The result, however, was an immediate acceptance of the manuscript by the prestigious medical journal.

Attached to the back of the reprint, by a paper clip, was a cutting from the English newspaper, The Daily Express. Richard smiled as he unfolded the fragile newsprint and saw the double column headed, "African Elephants May Change Your Diet." The commentary was a fairly good account of the work, until it reached the final statement: "These young doctors were amazed to see how many of these large animals had died of heart attacks." Richard chuckled as he remembered the response of his colleagues when they read the newspaper that day.

"Well, as least it was the only research of mine that reached the public press," he thought. "So much for fame and glory," and he shut the memorabilia away in a drawer where they belonged.

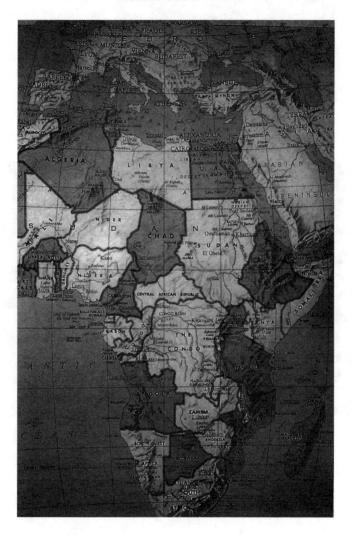

Africa

MARTIN GWENT LEWIS

AN UNUSUAL SAFARI

A safari in Africa usually conjures up in the minds of many people an organized trip through a game park in a van badly disguised as a zebra, or sitting in tents drinking gin and tonic under the moon, boasting about the lion that was almost shot earlier in the day. To the department of pathology in the medical school in Uganda in the 1960s, it presented quite a different prospect. My colleagues were always joking about how I would drop my duties and go off on a trip on any pretense. It was not exactly like that on this occasion.

The coffee break at 10:00 a.m. was a compulsory interlude in the workings of the day; the professor insisted on it, and explained that it was the one chance for all his staff to get together even for a brief few moments to exchange views and ideas, and to keep in touch.

On this particular occasion, the conversation came around to the study that I was supposed to organize between the Albany Medical School in New York and the University of East Africa. It had been noted by the professor's eminent predecessor, J.N.P. Davis, that aged-matched Africans had a much lower incidence of arteriosclerosis and atherosclerosis than their equivalents in New York. Therefore, hearts and portions of the coronary arteries were being shipped constantly in packages. Frankly, it wasn't the most exciting research project.

"I've got a great idea," I said, as I sat back with my coffee balanced on my knee, trying to light my pipe. I had the floor, since no one at that point had anything particular to say. "If we really want to find out whether diet is the cause of atherosclerosis, then what we need is another control study." At this point I noticed out of the corner of my eye that the professor showed a small spark of interest. "Such as what?" came the only response, from the corner of the room.

"Well, if one were to do autopsies on the Karamajong, surely that would be a great comparison." At this point I had the attention of the whole room. Some of them were smiling, but rather derisively. The professor was looking much more interested. Before anyone could shoot down the idea, I went on. "It is well known that the Karamajong live on a totally different kind of diet from the Bantus, which is the basis of our comparison study here. They don't live on high-carbohydrate diets, and they often, as you well know, drink the blood of their animals mixed with milk and urine." Everyone in the room who had been in East Africa for any reasonable length of time knew the ceremonial and cultural activities of this particular tribe in the far north of Uganda, who were genetically related to the Masai of Kenya.

The skeptic in the far corner of the room raised his head once more. "And how do you propose to do autopsies on people who live several hundred miles away in a restricted area of the country? Are you going to ask them to send bodies down here to Kampala? We're the only people who do autopsies, except for forensic cases."

He was right. Before I could answer, the professor rose

slowly to his feet and gazed out of the window. This was a signal that he was about to address us, and everyone in the room had the greatest regard and respect for this remarkable man, who not only ran the Pathology Department but was dean of the medical school and an inspiration to every one of us.

He turned on his heel. "Of course, there's one solution if this is a feasible project, and I'm beginning to think it might be," the professor said, "and that is for a team of people to go to the area. After all, there's a hospital there, and there's bound to be some kind of a mortuary we can use. What do you think, Frank?"

The man he addressed was the oldest member of the department, and looked even older since he had the white hair of his Scottish ancestry. Dr. Frank MacDonald had a remarkable experience in pathology, particularly autopsies. Before joining the department in Kampala, he had been the head forensic pathologist in Ghana for years. He was also quite used to doing autopsies in bizarre and outlandish places.

Frank drew on his inevitable and constant cigarette. "Well, I don't know, Michael," he said in his broad Canadian drawl. He was the only one of us who ever addressed the professor by his Christian name. The rest of us referred to him as "Prof," which was a term of respect and endearment at the same time. McDonald, however, was not British, did not have his career dependent upon the protocol of the British Medical School system, and was, in fact, older than the professor. They therefore had a somewhat different relationship.

We waited. Frank was not someone who spoke fast and

furiously, and he puffed away on his cigarette.

"Well, there's one way it could be done," he said, "and that's to make contact with the police."

Everyone in the room now had their attention fixed firmly on the gray-haired Canadian.

"Well, it's like this," he went on. "As you know, there are constant inter-tribal wars going on in that area, not only within Uganda, but over the border in Kenya with the Turkana tribe as well. The other fact that I'm sure many of you are aware of, or maybe you're not, is that the Karamajong do not bury their dead but leave them out in the field for the jackals and hyenas."

The point began to dawn on some of us.

"You mean, Frank," I interrupted, "that we would, as it were, go out searching after some kind of battle and do autopsies on dead bodies in the middle of the field."

"Well, dammit, man; you did that with elephants, didn't you?"

I shrugged. It was obviously different, to me at least.

"Well, if you go up there and expect to do autopsies in the hospital, you may have a great surprise, since the only ones you would see would be those that died in the hospital, and a lot of those Karamajong are not that obliging."

The professor turned to Frank. "Tell me, Frank, do you think this is worth our effort? It sounds like a good idea to me. After all, no one's done autopsies on this group of people -- ever, have they?"

"Not to my knowledge," Frank MacDonald replied. "It certainly has to be done at some point, and I think young Jones over here is the obvious man for the job."

At this my heart sank. Why had I not kept my big mouth

shut? I had other projects I was interested in, and I was throwing out this idea idly in the hope that someone else would pick up the slack in this otherwise tedious project of atherosclerosis. But, I had sunk my own ship.

The professor turned and said, "I think that's a great idea, Frank, but I want you to go with him."

Now it was MacDonald's turn to look glum, not that he objected to going off on safari -- he enjoyed it -- but I think he had some other plans, too, and being that far from home didn't always suit his purposes.

"Okay, Prof, if that's what you want. I'll contact the police and get some kind of authorization to do what we need to do, if young Jones over here will organize the personnel we'll need to take with us, and equipment, etc."

I realized that I was in the presence of very decisive men, particularly when other people's lives were being organized. It was too late to change their minds.

Immediately after coffee the activity started. To my amazement and delight, the mortuary attendant who ran our autopsy service at the hospital expressed a desire to come. He quite clearly understood that without him the project would be a total failure. Constanti, as his name was, and he was indeed worthy of his name, had been in that department since anyone could remember, and organized it like a military operation. He could do an autopsy quicker than any pathologist I've never met to this day, but he had never, ever, left his native Buganda, the country around the capital, Kampala, in his life, and no one knew quite how old he was.

Surprisingly, it took less than a week to get everything organized for the trip. There were to be three vehicles. MacDonald and a medical student from London on an elective were to travel in Frank's huge 4.5 liter black Woolsey. That was by far the most comfortable vehicle on the safari. The other one was a small Volkswagen with Seymour Volpers from the Harvard Medical School, who was doing research, as far as we could gather, on something quite unrelated, but took the opportunity of joining us. He was accompanied by a small, young-looking medical technician who followed him around everywhere and did his bidding. I was accompanied by Constanti and Ian Phillips, a bacteriologist from London, who was interested in everything and begged to be allowed to join us. Our vehicle was the old workhorse of the department, an old, indeed very old, long wheel based Land Rover, which was covered with scratches and dents and was thought to be probably the original model. It was loaded to capacity with the necessary equipment for our venture. This included bags of salt and formaldehyde to fix and preserve specimens, and various containers. There was just about enough room for the three of us to sit in the long bench seat in the front.

The plan was that we would travel on the hard top road which led to the Kenyan border, and then to the town of Mbale. During this stretch of the trip the poor old Land Rover would certainly be the slowest vehicle, and therefore we planned to set off earlier. The other two vehicles would, in turn, leave in some staggered fashion, almost like the handicap in a race. I sincerely hoped that the second leg of the journey through extremely rough country would somewhat reverse this handicap.

We set off along the road between Kampala and Jinja, traveling eastward toward the source of the Nile, and were all in high spirits. At every incline the poor old Land Rover had to be changed into bottom gear, but we made up for it by rolling down the hills on the other side. The road would not allow fast traffic anyway, since it was one of the most populous areas in Uganda. All along this fifty miles of hard surface road there were small villages and townships, and plantain groves, and always crowds of people waiting for local African buses or standing around for no reason that was apparent to anyone else. It was necessary to stop frequently to avoid running over goats and chickens, and even small children.

Despite all of this we made good time and were soon coming down the long sloping hill toward the town of Jinja. In the distance could be seen a thin ribbon of water: the Nile as it emerges from Lake Victoria. Constanti became agitated and made it clear that he wished to stop. I pulled up to the side of the road and he disappeared into the bush.

Phillips smiled and said to me, "Well, I suppose his bladder isn't as young as ours." But after twenty minutes of waiting, we both began to get a little worried. Then, out of the bush emerged Constanti, followed by three Africans with huge bundles of the green plantain, the matoke, which is the staple diet of the Bagandan tribe.

"Why on earth are you bringing that along?" I asked.

"Well, we must make sure that there's matoke for the rest of this trip."

"That's crazy, Constanti. It grows on the other side of the Nile in Busoga, and almost up as far as Karamoja. We don't have to load up at this moment."

"Ah, well, you see, this is the first time I have left Buganda. Once we cross over there into the land of the

29

Busoga tribe, how do I know they have matoke, or matoke worth eating?"

I remembered how important this staple diet, this almost tasteless plantain that they worshiped, was to the Bagandan. With a great deal of difficulty and reshuffling, we managed to get the great bundles into the back of the Land Rover, which was now impossible to see out of through the rear mirror.

As we crossed the bridge over the emerging Nile at Jinja, I saw the look of wide amazement in Constanti's eyes. It was indeed a magnificent sight, and Ian Phillips had not been there before either.

There through a long metal tube-like structure emerges the powerful White Nile, into an almost tumultuous fall into the valley below. Then the river appears to take off like a great roaring snake through the bushes and rock-strewn pathway into the distance, as if making up for the presumptuous restrictions of human hands.

The remainder of the journey was quite uneventful. The road from Jinja had a good surface, and within another two and a half to three hours we entered the pretty little town of Mbale, nestled on the western slopes of Mount Elgon. The great mountain could only be seen partially from our approach from the south, but even then it was spectacular. On the map it looked like a huge carbuncle sticking up out of the surrounding countryside and low rolling hills. It formed one of the natural boundaries with Kenya, which was just a few miles up the road.

Like many other African towns there were single-storied small dwellings of various shapes and sizes, and the inevitable plantations growing the green plantain, which I unkindly pointed out to Constanti.

As we drew into the hotel, there were well-manicured lawns, beautiful hibiscus hedges, and the sweet smell of the frangipanis, mingled with the smell of charcoal fires from somewhere in the distant hills. It had recently rained and the steam was rising from the pathway, and the whole atmosphere was clean and refreshing.

There, adjacent to the front entrance of the hotel, were the Volkswagen and the large, unmistakable black 4.5 liter Woolsey. It was not surprising, since they had overtaken us on the road some several hours before. We were ushered to our rooms, and arranged to meet in the bar before dinner.

Everything seemed to have gone well, no mishaps on the road, and we had all managed to arrive at this first evening's destination together, and looked forward to a very pleasant collective meal and discussion.

Then we encountered one of those strange anomalies in East Africa. The manager was an East African Indian who had been trained by the old British colonials to have certain standards, and he made no bones about applying them to the letter. As we stood outside of the dining room in a motley collection of outfits, he pointed out a notice over the door which must have been there for many years but was clean and polished. It announced that jackets and ties, or African national dress, must be worn.

This came as a bit of a blow, since several of us had not anticipated socializing in this kind of way when we planned the safari. I certainly hadn't brought any formal outfits of any description. I was wearing an old bush jacket and a pair of khaki shorts. Phillips was dressed in a very similar fashion, and McDonald had some atrocious multicolored checkered

31

jacket which only a Canadian or American would wear. Volpers, the Harvard man, was dressed in a classical safari outfit that he must have bought in some shop in Nairobi. The only one who was properly attired, of course, was Constanti, who appeared in a very nice suit with collar and tie. Only the Africans can match the Indians in terms of British convention. A quick Council of War dismissed the idea of attacking the Indian manager and tying him up and dumping him somewhere, however, MacDonald suddenly had an inspiration.

"Come with me, gentlemen," he said, and we paraded off to his room.

"They want jackets, collars and ties, and African national dress, do they? Well, let's figure this out, then," and he bundled through his suitcase, piling things on the bed.

I shall never forget the look in that Indian manager's eyes when we returned. I was wearing the horrible checked jacket of MacDonald's, which was several sizes too big and came down below my knees, and for a tie had taken a belt from somebody's bush jacket and made it into a tie, including the holes down the middle. Volpers had borrowed some kind of a tie from Constanti, and managed to arrange his bush jacket to look more respectable. It was McDonald who caused the poor man to nearly have a fit. He was standing there in some strange outfit that seemed to hang from his neck like a large bell tent, made of some shaggy cloth-like material, and on his head was a little white cap.

The man could barely sputter out the words, "What are you doing to me, sirs? What are doing to me?"

"Well," said MacDonald, "these gentlemen have got jackets and ties. Some of them are a little unusual, I grant you."

"Unusual!" the man said. "This is ridiculous. And what about you, sir? What do you think you're wearing?"

"Aha! I'm wearing the national dress of Ghana, of which I am an official honorary chieftain of the Ashanti tribe." The strange thing about it was that it was a true story. MacDonald had been given this honor during his days in West Africa.

The manager, almost exploding in frustration and anger, indicated that we should follow him, and he took us to a private dining room at the back of the hotel which was hurriedly made appropriate.

"Now why the hell couldn't he have done this in the first place," Volpers said, "and saved us all this carnival charade?"

"You don't understand these people, Seymour. This is as important to them as if they were running the Ritz Carlton in Chicago, and there's nothing you can do about it."

After several beers we all saw the humorous side of it and had a great evening. Even the frustrated manager finally came in and we managed to make him smile. We also achieved a certain amount of rapport with him by giving him a generous tip.

We set off early the following morning. By the looks of them, some of my colleagues had stayed up rather late celebrating. There was a great contrast in this particular part of the journey. We left behind us the lush green tropical vegetation and the road gradually, and then more rapidly, entered a more and more arid wasteland.

On our first day's journey, we could barely see more than a few yards from the road, and now the vista opened up as far as the eye could see, scrub land and desert, with a few small conical low-lying hills. To our right we passed alongside a ridge of mountains that seemed to merge into the horizon, but with not a tree to be seen.

The other tremendous contrast was that for several hours we saw no sign of life. There were none of the shouting, cheering African children at the roadside, or the usual goats and chickens. And then, quite abruptly, as we turned the bend in the road, standing like a statue was this tall, elegant-looking man with fine aquiline features and a huge headdress which appeared to be made of clay and feathers. Thrown over his left shoulder nonchalantly was a cloak, and in his right hand a twelve-foot spear. Apart from that he was totally naked.

I thought Constanti's eyes would pop out from his head. He stared in utter disbelief. "Is that a Karamajong?" he exclaimed.

I nodded.

"But these people are savages!" he shouted. "It's all your fault!"

"All my fault?" I said. "What on earth has it got to do with me?"

"I mean your people should have civilized them like us."

I wanted to laugh, but realized that Constanti was absolutely serious.

"I think you'll find, my old friend, that they don't want to be civilized, and I doubt very much if anybody is going to change them."

Constanti remained unconvinced.

A few miles farther up the road another similar individual appeared and made it very clear to us by the

34

waving of his hand that he wanted a lift. To Constanti's horror, we stopped, and the diminutive African jumped into the back seat. The tall Karamajong said nothing, looked at us, nodded his head, and sat between me and Phillips. We drove along for approximately half an hour, no one saying a thing. We tried to converse with him, but he did not respond. He sat looking straight ahead. I noticed that there was a series of tattoo marks on his right arm, and Ian noticed similar ones on the left.

Risking whether he understood English or not, I said to Phillips, "You know what those tattoo marks mean? Each one represents the number of people he's killed."

"Oh, hell. Is that right?" asked Phillips.

"Yeah. And I'm not sure, but I think the left arm means women and children, and the right arm means men. I sincerely hope that the ones on your side are no more than on mine, because he's got quite a few."

We sat back in silence. It evoked no response from the Karamajong at all, and Constanti sat huddled up in the back seat, his eyes wide with terror. And then quite suddenly the tall warrior nudged me and indicated we should stop. I pulled up at the side of the road, he got out, bowed his head and walked away with one wave of the arm, and disappeared into the scrub land, to wherever he was going.

"These are really amazing people, you must admit," Phillips said. Constanti made no reply.

The town of Moroto, which was the only town in the region of Karamoja, was quite different from anything that any of us had seen. There it was in the midst of a countryside that was rock-strewn desert with small thorny plants, and largely flat. The exception to this monotonous terrain was a circular mountain mass known as Mount Moroto, which stood abruptly in this flat, arid plain, with no other mountains within hundreds of miles. This was no small hill, it was several thousand feet high.

The town was quite a contrast from either Kampala or Mbale, consisting of a single street with a few broken-down Indian dukas. Even these resilient tradesmen were fewer in this desolate place. The only permanent buildings were the government rest house, the police station, and the hospital.

They were expecting us, and certainly our rooms, although rather Spartan, were clean, and there appeared to be a small sitting room with a verandah looking out across a hard-baked enclosure toward the road which bisected the small town. The hospital was just visible through a few thorn bushes on the other side of the road.

The atmosphere was so dry that it made all our eyes feel sore, and within a few hours everyone's nose was so painful that it was almost impossible to breathe without feeling excruciating pain at times.

That evening some kind of meat stew was served with rather old and tasteless vegetables. The meat was tough and had a horrible ability to stick to the teeth. Most of us spent about an hour after dinner trying to pick the fragments from out of our mouths. The thought of spending the next few weeks in this place was certainly depressing.

The following morning Frank MacDonald and I presented our credentials to the local chief of police. He was a large man with very dark, black shiny skin, clearly not a Karamajong, but by his features one of the members of the Bantu tribes. He must have been six foot four, and large in all proportions. He sat slumped over a desk, and although his uniform was smart and well kept, he had a weary look in his eyes. He read through the letter of introduction from the chief of police of Uganda, and then I tried to explain to him our project.

He looked up wearily from the letter. "It is very dangerous, doctors. I would advise waiting at the hospital for deaths, but you have the authority if you insist."

At this point, Frank MacDonald interrupted. "I've worked with the Royal Canadian Mounted Police and the north Ghanian constables, and I'm not afraid of a few spears."

The policeman sighed. "If it were only a few spears, doctor, I would not be afraid either. But two days ago we were attacked by a party of Turkana from the Kenya side of the border. There were 700 of them, with Land Rovers armed with mounted Bren guns, which they'd bought from the Somalis. They killed many of my men and shot down a helicopter. We're having a Council of War this week with our counterparts in the Kenyan police to try to settle this."

Even MacDonald sat in stunned silence. The tired looking policeman had made his point.

I didn't need any persuading that staying at the hospital was where we belonged.

The policeman seemed relieved, shook our hands and wished us success.

With our egos somewhat deflated, we wandered across to the hospital to introduce ourselves. We were met by a young Dutchman who said he was a dermatologist from Utrecht. His partners were another Dutchman, who was a pediatrician, and a Russian surgeon who was away somewhere on a trip. They were the only physicians in the entire Karamoja district.

I commented about how busy that this must be.

"Oh, not as much as you'd think," he said. "The Karamajong are resilient stoical people. They only come to the hospital when they're practically dead. I've seen them walk miles with a spear sticking through them. The only other major disease we get here, apart from war wounds, is smallpox."

"Looks like we could be here for quite a while to get enough cases to make any sense, at this rate," MacDonald said as we strolled back to the rest house.

I must admit, I hadn't thought of it in quite this light. We were so used to doing literally hundreds of autopsies at the main hospital in Kampala that I visualized a couple of weeks producing enough material to solve the problem one way or the other. When we inspected the mortuary it was immediately apparent that it had not been used in some time.

It's always interesting how inactivity always corrects itself at the most inappropriate time. That evening, while we were sitting and finishing dinner, a messenger rushed into the dining room and handed me a piece of paper, on which was written "body in morgue." I showed it around the table and everyone laughed.

"Well, looks like you're off to a good start," said MacDonald, indicating his reluctance to join me. Constanti, of course, leapt to his feet. There was no way in the world that he was going to allow me or anyone else to enter that morgue without his assistance.

The sun was just setting as we walked briskly along the hard baked ground of the narrow pathway that wound through the grounds of the hospital to a small, wooden, one-storied hut which looked as if it had not been painted for many years. Around the hut were small piles of whitish material which Constanti, to his horror, recognized as hyena dung. We were used to seeing vultures sitting on the mortuary at the main hospital in Kampala, but somehow the proximity of hyenas was a bit more inhibiting. We opened the door with the key that had been provided by the runner, and switched on the only light.

I'm not sure which of us was the more shocked, but Constanti expressed his disgust openly in a mixture of Lugandan and English. "This is the filthiest place I've ever seen. I am very sorry indeed that you will have to work in such filth. It is not fit for you and your colleagues."

There was a raw smell of death, and more -- the old, old smell of previous deaths. Pathologists throughout the world are not easily affected by bad aromas, but this was special. This was the ancient smell of the house of death. The very wood of the walls and tables seemed to be steeped in the concentrated juices of generations of bodies.

Lying on the table was a body. It did not appear to be a Karamajong, since this was an African dressed in European clothes with long khaki trousers, a bush shirt, and a pair of black shoes. There appeared to be an enormous wound in his left lower abdomen, and an equally nasty-looking wound above the right shoulder, and his throat had been slit from ear to ear, right down to the bone. Lying across the floor at the foot of the table was a twelve-foot long Karamajong spear, similar to the ones we'd seen carried by warriors on the road.

At this moment, MacDonald, who could not resist the temptation to see what we were up to, arrived and glanced at the body, taking in all of the facts in a flash.

39

"Well!" he said. "The cause of death looks pretty damned obvious to me. I'll leave you to it." With that he lit a cigarette and disappeared.

Although there was no humidity, it was still warm inside that building, so we stripped off to our waists, found some old rubber aprons, and took out our box of instruments that we had asked to be placed there earlier in the day. MacDonald, of course, was right. It didn't take long to establish the cause of death. The spear had clearly gone right through the abdomen, up through the diaphragm, and right lung. That alone would have killed several men, but for good measure his throat had been opened right down to the cervical vertebrae.

I noticed the man was wearing bicycle clips at his ankles. He had clearly been killed for his bicycle. Sure enough, as we expected, the heart, the aorta and the coronary arteries were as clean as that of a twelve-year-old child in England or America. On the other hand, we still hadn't solved any problems, since the man wasn't of the tribe that we were interested in in the first place.

We were almost finished, and both of us anxious to leave the place, which had a morbid air about it, even for pathologists, when there was a knock on the door. Constanti, who had been gradually building up a sense of anxiety throughout the course of the procedure, now jumped as if he was electrified. Seizing hold of a huge bone-cutter and the largest knife, he poised himself toward the door like some gladiator. I must admit, I was taken aback too. It was eight o'clock at night by now, and dark outside, and who of our group would have knocked?

Constanti's stance and attitude were infectious. I took

hold of a large knife, and we both approached the door, which I grabbed hold of and pulled open. There standing in the open doorway were a young African boy and girl, hand in hand.

"Good evening, sir," they said, to which Constanti screamed "What do you want? What are you doing here?"

You would have thought that a young courting couple, even if their curiosity overcame them, would have been terrified by the sight of these two men stripped to the waist, covered with blood-stained aprons, in the presence of a body, and carrying huge knives, and in an obvious antagonistic mood.

I'll never understand to this day, but they simply said, "Oh, sorry to disturb you. Good night, sir," and disappeared.

Constanti was not satisfied with my shrugging of the shoulders and walking back to the table. "It's a trap! It's a trap, doctor! Don't you understand? But we're surrounded by the Karamajong! They'll kill us for doing this."

I looked at him and tried to explain that this was not one of the Karamajong; that they probably killed the man in the first place, and didn't have the slightest interest in what we were doing. He was not convinced, so we hurriedly finished the job and literally ran down the pathway back to the guest house. I never felt so foolish in my life. When we told MacDonald and the others, we were the butt of their jokes and merriment for the rest of the evening. Constanti went to bed in disgust.

For the next three days, nothing of any note occurred. There were no emergencies at the hospital, and no bodies in the morgue, and no sign of any kind of activity. I had not been used to forced inactivity in a long time, and tried to write some notes on some papers that were overdue. The others became so bored that apart from Constanti they all took off on an expedition to visit one of the newest game parks on the northernmost border of Uganda.

After breakfast one morning, as I sat on the verandah of the rest house staring across at the hospital, Constanti came running up the steps, breathless. "Quick! Quick, doctor! You must come! Very serious...very serious indeed! Follow me, quickly!"

It was clear that I could get nothing coherent out of him, and so followed him across the grounds to the hospital. As we proceeded, he tried to piece together the reason for his anxiety.

"There is a small child, and this small child was guarding some strange beasts."

"Strange beasts?" I asked. "What on earth are you talking about?"

"Large beasts, with big mounds on their backs, and big ugly looking mouths. I saw one of them."

I suddenly realized that this short fat Bagandan from the shores of Lake Victoria was describing his first encounter with a camel.

I explained to him what they were, and he then said, "Well, it doesn't matter about the beasts. The terrible thing is that some Karamajong shot the child with an arrow, and he is lying in the hospital dying, and I cannot find any of the doctors."

I was somewhat taken aback. It had been a few years since I'd performed any surgery, or even looked after live patients, and I felt scared. But as I entered the ward and saw the poor child lying there, maybe ten or eleven years old, with two gaping wounds in which loops of intestine were hanging out, I realized that I was at least better than no one. I ordered the operating room to be gotten ready, and we managed to put up a drip in case we needed blood, although I had no idea how much blood they had in the hospital. I was about to consider what kind of incision to make when the Dutch dermatologist bustled into the operating room.

"Oh, thank you indeed. I am so grateful that you took over in my absence," and he glanced down at the child.

"Well," I said, "I'd be very happy to assist, if you'd like."

"Oh, yes. That would be a great help. Thank you very much. I'm really not much good at surgery, you know. I haven't done very much."

I looked aghast at what he then proceeded to do. He poked the intestines back into the wound and proceeded to suture them.

"Ah...excuse me, but..." and I hesitated, but felt obliged to point out to him that if an arrow had gone in through one side of the abdomen and come out through the other side, as clearly this had, that in between there was likely to be a great deal of damage, and that must be assessed and dealt with. He was not convinced.

Later that day I had the very sad duty of performing an autopsy on the child. It isn't very often that a pathologist autopsies a patient that he has been clinically involved with during life.

Sure enough I was right. A large section of intestine had been ripped by the arrow, including the main large bowel. I doubt very much, when I tried to rationalize it, that we could have done anything to try to save the child's life -- a pathologist who dabbled a little in surgery, and a dermatologist who had even less experience, were hardly a team in the middle of this far-flung spot to do major gastrointestinal surgery, but I still felt terribly that we hadn't tried. It haunted me for days.

"After all," I kept reminding myself, "I came up here to do autopsies, not to substitute for the surgeons who disappeared."

Two days later I had a second opportunity. Once again it was not a call to the morgue, but to the ward. On this occasion it was an adult male African in his forties, who had been attacked, not by the Karamajong, but by some drunken members of the Uganda armed forces. His abdomen exhibited the board-like rigidity that indicated something inside had been ruptured. Once again, the Dutch dermatologist arrived, and having assessed the situation proceeded to make a tiny incision in the upper mid-abdomen. As we both predicted, blood came out, confirming that something inside had ruptured.

At this point he was about to sew up, when I felt the strong conviction to interfere.

"I'm terribly sorry, but I wonder if you'd mind if I continued."

"Well, I was going to send him to Mbale. You know, we can't deal with this kind of surgery here, not without our Russian surgeon being back."

"I think the fellow will die long before he gets to Mbale. I'd like to have a shot at this."

"Oh, I'd be delighted. By all means, please go on," he said without any rancor.

The problem of which incision to make had already been

44

made for me, to some extent, so I continued his small midline incision, right down the middle of the abdomen as far as I could go. This is the classical autopsy incision, and I wondered as to the validity of what I was doing, but since I had no idea what was ruptured, it seemed logical. Shortly after, there was a great deal of blood. We mopped it up, we put hot packs in, and to everyone's delight the blood pressure stabilized, and the patient seemed to be doing all right. Once I got inside the abdomen, my anxiety, to some extent, disappeared. I had as a pathologist over the previous few years opened up many hundreds of abdominal cavities, and I knew my way around fairly instinctively. I hoped it was the spleen that was ruptured since I felt that I could remove that without too much trouble. Unfortunately, the spleen was intact. My heart sank at the thought of the kidneys being the site of the problem, since I felt totally inadequate to remove a kidney through an anterior abdominal incision. And then, I saw the problem. The liver had been literally torn in half. There was an enormous wound extending through the full thickness of the organ, with blood oozing out in fairly considerable quantities. Once again, we packed the area tightly, and the bleeding temporarily stopped.

I suppose I would have been within my rights to have said, "That's it," and sewed him up, and accepted defeat, but somehow I couldn't. And so, I turned to one of the African assistants and said, "Do you have one of those big curved needles -- I've forgotten the name?"

"Oh, yes." They handed me the instrument. I made some kind of a mattress suture across the gaping wound, and packed it with some absorbent coagulant gauze material, which luckily they had.

45

We finally took out the packs and stood back. The bleeding had stopped. Everyone in the operating room cheered. I felt acutely embarrassed. Now facing me was to re-suture that enormous incision I'd made, which took considerably longer than the whole procedure up to that point. The patient stabilized, and I walked slowly back, smoking my pipe, through the grounds of the hospital back to the rest house.

The following morning I had the delight and reward of standing at the side of the bed while the man, smiling and very much alive, grasped my hand and expressed his gratitude. As I walked away, I thought, Well, I'm a real doctor after all. I was grateful for that chance.

A week later, we were prepared to leave and return to Kampala. We had not achieved very much, and were unlikely to do any better. I walked back into the ward to say farewell to my favorite patient. I saw the figure of a European standing at the foot of the bed while others were taking off the dressings, and realized this must be the Russian surgeon. I was about to quietly leave when someone noticed me and pointed, and they then indicated I should join them. He clicked his heels and said his name was some unpronounceable, and therefore totally forgettable, Russian-sounding name, and I told him mine.

"Hmmm," he said in his broken English. "Ruptured liver. Very difficult case."

"Yes," I said hesitantly. "Very difficult case, in fact."

"Where you from?"

I said, "Oh, from the medical school in Kampala."

"Ah. Hmmm. Department of surgery?"

"No. Well, actually department of pathology."

I saw the puzzled look on his face.

"Actually my patients don't usually do as well as this," I said.

There was no response.

I made my farewells, and smiling to myself left and joined the others.

Before the company returned to Kampala, we were given a unique opportunity. A missionary nurse whom we'd met at the hospital asked if we'd like to spend an evening in a Karamajong donga. These native villages were places that few visitors ever went to, but she knew the local chieftain and spoke their language fluently. Our contribution to the evening was to provide a goat for food.

The village was a large one by Karamajong standards, being the home of the paramount chief of the Mathanika tribe. The old man met us before we entered. He spoke a smattering of English. The village was certainly different from anything I'd seen in other parts of the country. The collection of conical-shaped huts was surrounded by huge dense thicket fence, over twelve feet high. There was only one way in or out, and each person had to crawl on their hands and knees to enter the enclosure. The chief explained to us that this was a protection against invaders, since it was difficult to make a mass attack through one small hole. Unfortunately, however, it also worked in reverse. He explained through the nurse interpreter and his own smattering of English how warriors from the various tribes would make a feint attack at drawing off the fighting men, then others would burn the circular fence, and then spear or club the women, children and old men as they attempted to escape through the only exit.

After this somewhat depressing introduction to the lifestyle of the people, we each crawled through the entrance into the enclosure, which consisted of hard baked ground and huts which almost touched each other. There must have been nearly twenty of these structures, and some larger ones which appeared to be storage areas. The cattle were kept in a separate corral close to the village. One of the tragedies of these people and their constant inter-tribal warfare was that no one dared to use the only safe grazing between the various tribal areas. They were, therefore, always on the brink of losing their cattle, and any drought resulted in a total tragedy.

The chief sighed and explained that if only they could cooperate together they could solve most of their problems. I must admit, in my few years in East Africa this seemed to be the tragedy of Africa as a whole.

The nurse turned to us and said, "But on the other hand, the chief wants to assure you that you're in no danger. No Karamajong would dare to touch a white man. The last time that happened, years ago..."

The old man at this point was pointing at the sky. "Men came out of the sky and floated down to earth with guns."

"Oh, British paratroopers," MacDonald exclaimed.

"Yes, I suppose that must have been a pretty impressive shock to them," Phillips interjected.

The nurse, on behalf of the chief, pointed out to us that if we wished to we could sleep anywhere we liked on the open ground, and even in those no man's lands between the tribal areas since they were sure that if any one of us were harmed those men would come down out of the sky again.

"Yes," grunted Seymour Volpers, the Harvard man, "it's one thing to attack women and children and burn their houses down, and it's another to face submachine guns and paratroopers."

None of us felt like commenting. It didn't seem appropriate.

Luckily, the mood of the evening changed abruptly as the various warriors of the tribe came to greet us. What a sight: these tall, muscular-looking men with their huge plumed head-dresses made of baked clay and feathers, leaning nonchalantly on their huge spears. They towered above all of us, but greeted us with beaming smiles, although with a certain shyness. They were clearly not used to having visitors in their village. In fact, none of us felt quite at ease at first. There was something missing, a tremendous gap of tradition and background between the motley assorted group of white people and these tall, arrogant-looking Africans. I wondered what old Constanti would have thought of all this. He was not invited, and in any case made it quite clear that he would not attend.

The chief and the nurse went into conference, and then we were all instructed to sit around in a circle, in which there was a small fire burning. It was already beginning to get dark, and in that part of the country it cooled off quite rapidly after the sun went down. A huge chipped enamel bowl was produced from out of the darkness somewhere, and brought around by one of the chief's assistants. Each one of us was instructed to take a piece from the bowl.

I looked at it through the glow from the fire and the last embers of the setting sun. It contained rather nondescript

49

white meat; in fact, it was goat that had been boiled. There were, of course, no plates, no knives and forks, and we simply chewed on the meat, holding it in our hands. It was probably one of the most tasteless pieces of meat I've ever encountered, and as tough as the Karamajong beef that we'd been living on for the past few weeks. It had, in addition, a sort of rubbery consistency, which made it incredibly difficult to bite pieces off the bone.

Shortly following this, we received a handful of what looked like white porridge; in fact, it was posho, one of the few carbohydrate staple diets of the Karamajong, and made from sorghum, and even more tasteless than the meat.

I sat back and leaned on the ground, placing my piece of meat close to me, when a small dog crept out from one of the nearby huts. I quickly in the dark shoved the piece of meat toward him, which he seized hold of with great speed, and disappeared into the shadows. He didn't appear to like the posho as much as the meat, unfortunately. Feeling pleased with myself, I sat upright, and then to my horror, the chief, noticing that I'd apparently finished my food, insisted on seconds. This time the dog did not come to my aid.

The conversation was somewhat restricted, mainly because none of us could understand each other's languages, and since the company was scattered around in a circle it was difficult to talk to anyone except for the person immediately adjacent to oneself. The main reason, however, was that we were so busy trying to bite and chew the meat, and swallow the posho, that conversation would have been somewhat restricted anyway.

Finally, the food was either eaten or removed, and then another large enamel bowl started to be passed around the circle. Luckily, it was so dark by then that it was impossible to see what was actually in the bowl. From observing those to my right, I noticed that it was the custom to lift it to one's lips and take a drink.

The nurse leaned across to me and said, "This is the local Karamajong drink. Please don't offend them by not accepting it."

I nodded and bravely took the bowl to my lips, and with my teeth clenched squeezed some of the fluid reluctantly into my mouth. It was horrible. It tasted like a combination of vinegar and cold tea, and there was obviously particulate matter floating in it, which I spat from my clenched teeth. The chief seemed to be well pleased, and the bowl was passed around. All was going very well until it reached the man from Harvard. Seymour blatantly refused to accept the drink, and to our horror and disgust, particularly MacDonald's, he took a plastic cup from his pocket, and a hip flask, and poured himself his own drink.

The look on the chief's face, even in the dim light of the fire, was not very pleasing. Nevertheless, the bowl continued around and all the rest of us imbibed. The second time around the drink didn't seem quite so bad, and by the third time everyone was beginning to unwind. It was obvious that like any alcoholic beverage it was having its effect on the group collectively as well as individually.

This time I took the bowl boldly to my lips, and was about to take a large draft, when a beam of light broke through the darkness right across the bowl. Seymour Volpers, cursing and giving out numerous oaths, was apparently searching for his plastic cup, which someone or something had stolen. I was about to laugh with the others, since it seemed like poetic justice, until my eyes looked down into the bowl. Now I realized what I'd been drinking. It was filled with a kind of a muddy sludge-looking material in which there were obvious flies, and goodness knows what else, floating in it. My resolve was for a moment greatly disturbed, but gritting my teeth once more, and cursing Volpers under my breath, I took as much of a drink as I could manage.

The effect of this flowing bowl was that the whole company changed its attitude. There was a sudden warmth, not only from within but emanating from everyone, and spontaneously, one by one, the Karamajong warriors leapt to their feet, and with a kind of rhythmic chant began to jump up and down in the air.

"This is going to be a real treat," said the nurse. "They're going to do some Karamajong dancing for you, something they don't normally do in front of strangers."

There of course were no musical instruments, not even drums as the Buganda tribes, and all the other tribes of Uganda, would have used; simply the rhythmical chanting of the warriors as they jumped vertically into the air. It was a mesmerizing sight in the light of the fire to see these tall men leaping with great skill and with a rhythm that eventually took hold of one.

Whether it was the atmosphere created, or the drink, or both, I couldn't resist it, but leapt to my feet and started to try to mimic them. At first the nurse looked horrified and tried to restrain me, but then MacDonald got up as well, and Phillips, and before we could stop ourselves we were joining in. Instead of the warriors being offended, or upset, they gathered around us looking down and patting us on the head, as if we were small children, and all of their reserve seemed to melt away. Their smiles became real and human, and we were one of them. It was a marvelous feeling. How long we did it for I have no idea. It seemed to go on for hours, but no one cared. Even Seymour Volpers enthusiastically joined in, and exonerated himself.

Late into the night, or maybe early the following morning, when we, reluctantly this time, left the small Karamajong donga, I am sure all of us felt that we had left some friends behind.

The safari returned to Kampala, and we discussed the pros and cons of our venture. It became clear that we'd made no great strides in the understanding of atherosclerosis or the effect of diet on that disease, but I at least had had an opportunity to prove to myself that I was still some kind of a physician. We had also made contact with those strange shy people who are at the heart of Africa.

Mother and son

54

THE LAKE

EDWARD HOTEL

"I don't like the look of this place," Swenson said softly in his clipped Norwegian accent.

"Oh, let's not judge the place before we've had a look inside," Richard exclaimed.

The middle-aged, tall fair-haired Viking-looking man looked down at his young companion, who was considerably smaller. "Always the eternal optimist," he said.

Richard laughed. "Well, we've traveled a long way today, and if we can stay here for the night it certainly would be preferable to another two hours' drive, and even then to arrive in the dark at a very expensive game lodge."

Swenson was not convinced. They both looked at their other companion, a large rather portly young man with rosy cheeks, and a total look of innocence about him. He simply shrugged his shoulders, clearly not wishing to join in the argument.

They were standing by the Land Rover, staring across at a strange building indeed. The sign post which hung precariously at a crooked angle read 'Lake Edward Hotel.'

There were some rather dilapidated steps leading up to a verandah, and the whole building seemed to shimmer in the late afternoon African sun. The three of them had certainly traveled long and hard that day, bouncing along the red dirt roads of Uganda in a Land Rover that must have been one of the original models, and had long since lost most of its suspension. They were tired, were covered with dust, and parched with thirst. Richard ached from head to foot. Swenson appeared to be the one who was the least concerned about his state, but then he was, after all, a Norwegian and had been a partisan as a small boy in the mountains of Norway, fighting the Germans.

Richard, who was much younger, had spent his youth safely hidden from the rigors of the war in a small village in South Wales. In any case, he couldn't remember it. The smiling faced youth was a medical student from Yale University, who was far more intelligent than his appearance would indicate. In fact, he had a remarkable sense of humor, and between him and Richard they had invented a crazy form of shorthand talking which left the poor Norwegian totally confused during the length of the journey.

"This is a B-plus-mazing place, Richard, don't you think?"

"Oh, no, no," Richard said. "This is almost an A-minus-mazing place." They both laughed.

Swenson shrugged his shoulders in disgust."Let's go inside and see if we can find someone." He was a surly kind of individual, but a tremendous asset to have on any kind of journey. Nothing seemed to upset him except on that previous day.

Richard smiled as he remembered the look on Arne's face

when he saw the beautiful nun in the hospital in Fort Portal. For the next hour he was heard mumbling to himself, "What a waste, what a waste...a woman like that needs a man like me," and the others were almost afraid to laugh because he was clearly serious.

They entered the foyer of the hotel, if it could be graced with such a name, and heard the low hum of flies and a squeaking noise that indicated some kind of a ceiling fan, which was at least moving. The place had a complete air of degeneration. Everything was covered with dust, and there were no flowers in any flower pots and no paintings on the wall.

"It looks deserted to me," said Swenson, "and has been for a long time, I'll bet."

They were about to leave when a sleepy-looking African in dirty khaki shorts and a ragged shirt appeared from somewhere in the back of the hotel.

"Jambo, Bwana," he mumbled in Swahili.

"Jambo, Habari," Richard responded. "Where's the Bwana Mkubra?"

"You wait here, sirs. I will fetch."

"I think we should leave now," said Swenson.

Richard was anxious to explore further, and hesitated. He was about to follow his colleagues when a short, fat man in a stained grayish colored shirt and shorts appeared in the doorway.

"My name is Stavros, and I am the owner of the Lake Edward Hotel," he said proudly with a beaming smile on his face. His accent was European -- Greek, Richard thought. He extended his hands in greeting, and his smile broadened, revealing yellow discolored teeth. "The place has seen better

57

days, you understand. We don't get so many guests as in the old days of the British rule, and before they opened that cursed game lodge down the road from here."

A look of anxiety crossed his face as he glanced among the three travelers one at a time, as if to assess how far they'd come and how far they might go.

"Perhaps you would like to stay the night?" he asked anxiously.

Swenson took a quick step toward the door.

"It will be very dark by the time you reach the game lodge, and it's very expensive there," he went on with a sly grin crossing his face. "And after that, there's nothing for hundreds of miles. The road is dangerous at night."

They hesitated just enough for him to quickly resume his attack.

"The rooms alone at the game lodge will cost you more than 100 shillings a night. The food is typical tourist rubbish and costs more. Yet, on the other hand, I will give you a room each, dinner and a special breakfast at my house. And...." he stopped for a moment and rubbed his fingers, "I'll throw in a bottle of retsina for dinner tonight. And all of this will cost you -- what, a mere twenty shillings each."

Even Swenson hesitated at this point, and the Greek pressed on further with his arguments.

"I will return in fifteen minutes. You have a nice cold beer meanwhile, on the house. And look around. If you decide to stay, hokay. If you do not stay, you go to Queen Elizabeth Game Lodge, no hard feelings." He bowed courteously and withdrew.

They sat down on some battered old chairs, and a table was found in the corner, and on it was placed three reasonably cold beers, with labels indicating that they had been around for a long time, but in the guests particular state the beer tasted wonderful.

It was a sly and cunning move on the part of the Greek to realize their needs, and he allowed them just enough time to talk among themselves, very briefly.

Having drunk most of his beer, Swenson leaned back and said, "I must admit, twenty shillings is pretty good."

David, the student, smiling as usual, appeared to be as fascinated by his surroundings as he'd been anywhere they'd been on the trip, and simply nodded his approval.

The old Greek shuffled back into the room, and was so elated when they told him that they had decided to stay that he insisted on them having another drink on the house.

During the consumption of the second beer, they were presented by the short African they'd met earlier with what appeared to be the hotel register. A quick look at it made them realize that there hadn't been other guests for over a year. Despite that, they still decided that the decision had been made and would be kept.

Swenson rose to his feet, stretched, and said, "Well, I think I'd like to see my room and have a bath before dinner."

"Ah, now," the little Greek became quite agitated, "that it is a...not such a good idea, I think. Look, there is one hour left before sunset, and I will tell you just down the road here you will see elephant, and lion, all the game that you would spend days seeing in the game park. I know, I have lived here many years. This is a better way, then when you come back we will have dinner, and then you can relax."

"That's a great idea," said David. "I'd love to do that."

Richard joined in and agreed.

59

Swenson reluctantly and suspiciously walked away with them toward the Land Rover. "That's a strange little man," he said as they drove down the road, following his instructions. "Well, we might as well make the most of it now."

Sure enough, within that hour they saw a multitude of game, and all of their misgivings drifted away in the sheer delight of seeing groups of elephants, and even a pride of lions sitting at the side of the road, almost as if Stavros had put them there on display. They returned in a great mood, and were immediately greeted by the small Greek, who now had a different colored, but almost as dirty, shirt, and on the table were glasses and a bottle of whiskey.

"Well, was I not right?"

They admitted that it had been a wonderful, short and quite fulfilling trip.

"Now let us drink."

Richard had a good reputation and ability for being a talker; after all, he was from Wales. Swenson certainly was no great conversationalist, and David spent most of his energy smiling and agreeing with everything. Stavros was a real talker, and he dominated the conversation entirely and completely. He told stories with the most animated descriptions, in the course of which an almost complete bottle of whiskey was consumed, mostly by the Greek. At one point Richard wondered whether they would ever get any food at all, and whether this was just some bluff on the hotelier's part.

They were finally taken into the hotel dining room. It looked a bit different in candlelight, almost romantic, very dark, and only one small table just big enough for the four of them. They didn't realize at the time that the candlelight was not for effect, but for necessity, since the generator had temporarily broken down. Stavros assured them, however, that it was being fixed even while they would be having their dinner.

What was perhaps the most amazing of all was the food. They were served several large quantities of delicious Greek food that Richard had never seen the like of before. There were olives and dates, and all sorts of things that he couldn't imagine they would be able to get in Kampala, let alone out here in the middle of nowhere. The meal was washed down with the promised bottle of retsina, which must have been a precious commodity to the Greek.

After dinner they retired to the verandah, and began to smoke their pipes, and yet again, the Greek joined them with another bottle of whiskey.

Late into the night, Stavros told them his life story. He recalled his numerous African wives and concubines, one of whom he boasted was a princess. He told the stories with great conviction, but Richard wondered how much truth there really was in them. David was completely taken in, as usual, and seemed to hang on every word the old Greek said.

Eventually Swenson indicated that he'd had enough, and rose and asked if he could be led to his room.

Stavros reluctantly discontinued a great story about hunting in the hills with his African father-in-law, and with the aid of the diminutive African attendant who appeared to be the only other person in the hotel, they were led to their rooms by the light of a kerosene lamp. The generator, unfortunately, had still not been repaired.

"But do not worry. There will be a lamp placed in each of your rooms, and it is too late now anyway for bathing, and

61

all that sort of nonsense," said the Greek.

Swenson began to look irritated again, but the whiskey had had at least some mellowing effect on him, so he shrugged and grunted. The three moved into their respective rooms along a corridor at the back of the hotel.

It was just as well. Even in the semi-darkness the place looked like a pigsty. The room was covered with dust and smelled of damp and mildew. Richard was almost afraid to sleep in the bed, and decided to sleep on it instead. When he walked across by the dim light of the kerosene lamp to see a small wash basin in the corner, and turned the tap, nothing but dust came out of it. He laughed. "The old Greek's a cunning sod," he said. "He knew very well if we saw these rooms while we were still sober, and still capable of moving, that we would never have stayed." The effects of the whiskey and the wine, the good food, and the long hard day had their effects. He fell down on the creaking bed and was soon completely asleep.

It took something considerable and extremely noisy to awaken Richard at the best of times, and in his exhausted state it certainly would have been difficult; however, the noise that tore him from his deep slumbers was something the like of which he had never heard in his life. He sat up on the edge of the bed, realizing he was still clothed, and tried to make out the cause of the cacophony that he heard from outside. There seemed to be drums beating, and the sound of metal against metal. At one point he thought he heard the sound of a badly played trumpet, and then, to his horror, the obvious discharge of some fairly powerful firearms. In between all of this there was a great deal of shouting and yelling from what seemed like an enormous number of people. And then, the strangest of noises, the great trumpeting bellowing sounds, and the crashing of vegetation. As much as he wanted to know exactly what was going on, he didn't have the courage to venture from the room. Not only that, but it was pitch black, the kerosene lamp having gone out, and he had no idea how he would find his way out of the room, along the corridor, even if he wanted to. He sat hunched up on the bed and waited, and waited. It seemed like an eternity, but eventually the sounds dissipated as if they were gradually going off into the distance.

I wonder if I should go and find out what the others think, he thought. Once again, he leaned back on the bed, and in the process of trying to make up his mind he fell once again into a deep sleep.

The early light of dawn filtered through the dusty window and rips in ragged curtains. Richard shook himself, rubbed his hand on his unshaven chin, and realized that he was still in his clothes from yesterday. He decided that since he couldn't wash either, what was the point of changing his clothes? Somewhat miserably, he opened the door and made his way along the murky corridor, and once again came into the foyer.

There were Swenson and the young American sitting there, looking equally glum.

"What did you make of all that last night?" Richard asked.

"About an A-plus-mazing, I thought," David continued.

Swenson looked at him with a grimace. "Well I'm glad both of you had the good common sense not to get up and investigate," Swenson said. "Goodness knows what the heck was going on out there last night. We're lucky to be alive, if you ask me."

Richard shrugged his shoulders and sat down in the seat. "Well, I sure could do with a cup of coffee and some breakfast, and then maybe we can figure things out. I don't know about you fellows, but I haven't even had a chance to have a wash or change, or anything."

The look on Swenson's and David's faces indicated that they were in the same predicament.

Richard went over to the reception desk to ring the bell, but that didn't work. Eventually the sleepy African attendant shuffled into the room, looking even sleepier than usual.

"Sirs, you are invited to the Bwana's house for breakfast. I will show you the way."

As they walked out of the hotel and down the steps, Richard asked, "What was all that commotion and noise last night? I thought there was a flipping war going on."

"Oh, hah! Oh, elephants, as usual."

"Elephants!" Richard exclaimed. "I didn't hear any elephants." Then he stopped for a moment, and remembered the sound that he couldn't make out, the trumpeting and bellowing. "Of course, elephants! What on earth are elephants doing here, and why all the sounds of battle?" Richard continued.

"Ah, every night this happens," said the man. "Drove them off this time, sir," he said proudly.

It was clear that the servant wasn't going to give them any more information, and they wound around back of the hotel, and a short distance down the road. There was a sight indeed. The Greek's house looked more like an ancient Celtic fortress, with an enormous moat, behind which was an earthwork, higher than the tallest man. The three of them were speechless, and followed the African across a small drawbridge, through the earthworks, into an enclosure that took them even more by surprise. Here indeed was a small piece of the Mediterranean. There were figs and vines on a charming whitewashed house, from which came the strong smell of coffee.

Stavros appeared on the doorstep and rushed to welcome them with his arms held wide. "I hope you slept well, gentlemen. My poor hotel is not very comfortable, I'm afraid. With good Greek coffee and breakfast we'll fix everything." He smiled widely, showing his yellow teeth.

Over the small cups of strong sweet coffee, Swenson finally raised the question of the noise.

"Oh, those damned elephants!" Stavros snarled. "I am constantly at war with the beasts. They try to destroy my house, my figs, my grapes. Why do you think I live surrounded by walls and moats?"

None of them knew what to say. Richard felt like laughing, but the serious look on the Greek's face stopped him in his tracks.

Hours later, as they bounced along the dirt road back to Kampala, Richard's mind kept returning to the animated Greek host at the Lake Edward Hotel. In fact, for years after that, every time he smelled Greek coffee, or as the Turkish call it -- Turkish coffee, or the Armenians -- Armenian coffee, or the Arabs -- Arabic coffee, he wondered why it was that a man would leave his native land and settle in such an obscure wild spot, growing his grapes and his figs, and fighting off the marauding elephants night after night. I wonder if he really was married to a princess, Richard thought.

Eighteen months later, Richard was in the throes of packing. He was leaving Uganda for England. Although there was a certain sadness, there was also a sense of great relief. He was interrupted in his chores by the announcement that a neighbor had arrived to say good-bye. To Richard's great surprise, Father Donahue entered the room.

"My dear young friend, I'm sorry that you're leaving, but times here are very sad right now."

Richard extended his hand, and the large elderly man with graying hair, dressed in the long white garb of the White Fathers, shook it strongly and almost painfully.

Richard was not a member of the Catholic church, but in company with everyone else had the greatest respect for this order of the White Fathers. They had made a great impact on the life of Ugandans, and were devoted to their cause. Richard had barely met the old man except at occasional cocktail parties. The White Fathers were famous for their attendance at such gatherings. He was, therefore, somewhat surprised that he would have taken the trouble to have come and said good-bye.

"I won't beat around the bush," said Father Donahue, "but those of us who must remain here will have some difficult tasks ahead, one of which will be to find safe havens for various members of the Buganda tribe who will undoubtedly become the target of our friend, General Amin. I know you've traveled widely through this country, and have made many friends. What I need to know desperately is...can you tell me some places where, if the necessity arises, and I'm afraid it will, where we can send some African families where Idi Amin's troops will be less likely to find them? I'm looking for the sort of place that's maybe close to the borders where we can easily get them out."

Richard sat down on one of the packing cases, taken completely by surprise.

"Well, Father. There is, of course, the Mission Hospital in Amoudat, close to the Kenyan border, and...Palo Corti's Mission up in Gulu, but..." then it struck him. "Oh, Father, I know the perfect place!"

Richard sifted idly through his morning mail. He recognized the stamps of Uganda on a battered-looking old brown envelope. It was almost a year since he had left Kampala, and until a few weeks prior to that day, correspondence had been sparse. As he opened the envelope he realized that it had none of the official documentation from the University of East Africa that he was accustomed to seeing. The letter contained within was on a non-headed scrap of poor quality paper.

"Dear Dr. Jones -- You will no doubt remember our conversation the day you left Kampala. Your advice turned out to be correct -- the accommodation was perfect. Several friends unknown to you send their thanks. By the way, the proprietor thanks you for the referral of customers, and the bottle of retsina. He asked me to reassure you that on your next visit, which he hopes will not be too long, the water and electricity will be working. Apparently the elephants are still a problem -- whatever that means. Thank you again. Yours, Fr. Donahue."

Richard smiled, and then began to laugh as he pictured that fortified house behind the moat and the short fat Greek shaking his fist defiantly at nature and his foes.

The lone male

A ROAD

TO REMEMBER

There is something about certain stretches of road which one can never forget. I'm sure everyone can remember, sometimes quite vividly, a particular bend or twist, or the rise of a hill, and even recall the dappling effect of the light through the trees, or the glare from the surface. The reason for the remembrance often becomes obscure, and yet those few yards of a particular roadside stay in one's memory. There is one particular road I shall never forget. In fact, it changed my life.

The sun was low on the horizon; there was barely an hour left before dark. I slowed the old Ford Consul and shifted down into second gear as we approached the small township of Nakasongola. It was surprising to see so many people about the streets. Normally at that time of day in a sleepy African town of this small size, one would barely have seen anyone.

Angela stirred, and then quite suddenly sat bolt upright. There were scores of men marching down both sides of the road, carrying shields and waving spears and bush knives, and chanting some sort of African military air, or so it seemed.

"I don't like the look of this," she said.

"Oh, don't worry. It's probably some festival they're all going to. You know what Ugandans are like -- any excuse for a party," I said, and leaned out of the window and waved at some of the passersby.

We were almost through the town, and I was about to accelerate in anticipation of seeing the end of the street approaching, when a couple of East African Indians leapt out in front of the car, waving and shouting.

"Silly buggers," I muttered, and swerved to miss them. "What the dickens do they think they're up to?"

Angela looked anxiously at the two small children in the back seat of the car, who were both still fast asleep.

I squeezed her arm. "Are they okay?"

"Oh, yes," she sighed, and sat back down, but still had an anxious look about her that I had not seen in the short space of time I had known her.

I glanced at my watch. "Within half an hour we'll be on the good road, and in just over an hour we'll be in Kampala," I said cheerfully. "Don't worry. Your concerns will soon be over, and you'll be able to deliver the two little children to their family as you promised."

She smiled, and those deep green eyes once again almost mesmerized me. I had to look away to control the car. And then, quite out of the blue, as we turned a steep bend there appeared to be a group of men working across the road. I slammed on the brakes and changed the gear down to reinforce the stopping capacity of the car, and came to a halt in a cloud of dust. They appeared to be a cutting a trench, and a deep one at that, across the road, working from each side. It had not been completed, so the two ends of the trench did not meet in the middle, and there was just about enough road left for a car to pass. However, there was a double row of stones arranged on both sides of the trench, causing a complete obstruction.

Angela's face tensed and her lips became tight, and she clenched her fists.

Without thinking about the consequences, I jumped out of the car. "Get those damned stones out of the way. I've got to get to Kampala before dark," I started to shout. The men stopped and stared at me in silence. After a few minutes, a taller older man mumbled something to the others in what sounded like Luganda. It certainly was not Swahili. They began to move the stones from the road.

Without waiting for any other explanation, I jumped back into the car and drove through the gap.

"What an incredible piece of damned tomfoolery," I said to Angela as we began to accelerate up the slight hill away from the men and their roadwork. She said nothing, but stared intently ahead.

We came over the brow of the hill, and the road then took another sharp bend. This time I braked the car with such fury that we slid sideways into a pile of red dirt. The sight in front of us was startling. The entire road was blocked by a huge barrier of trees and bushes, and wooden stakes, that must have been fifteen or twenty feet high. Before I could gather my wits, dozens of men came from behind the barricade screaming and yelling, and waving spears and shields.

"Let's get out of here quickly," Angela shouted, with a

definite note of authority. The two little black children in the back seat had now woken up and were crying.

I threw the old Ford into reverse and drove backward as fast as I'd ever driven a car in that gear before, or since. I made enough distance between us and the pursuers to turn the car and head back up the road as fast as I could move it. As we came down the hill once more, I was vividly reminded that we were now between two barriers, for the men with the road works had replaced the stones, and this time stood defensively behind them with no obvious intention of removing them a second time.

I had been warned by others during my short stay in East Africa that sometimes quite elaborate robberies did take place on some quiet back roads, but this was the main road from Kampala to the most popular game park in Uganda. I had never heard of anyone being robbed on that road, and certainly this was a very elaborate and highly organized affair.

Before I could reason any further, Angela jumped out of the car, barely before I could stop it, and walked across to the men behind the rows of stones. All I heard were the Swahili words "Bwana," and "Totos." As I approached her closer, I could hear her, both in English and in Swahili, remonstrating with the older man about the lives of these children, and that we had nothing to do with whatever was going on, and surely small children, the little "Totos," would not be victims. It certainly struck a chord with the older man, who turned out to be one of the local Saza chiefs.

One of the faults Ugandans do not have is cruelty toward children. They have a high sense of family, and the idea of harming young children is highly offensive to the average

Ugandan male. Quickly he gave orders, and the men began to roll away the stones. Meanwhile, we could see the crowd of spear-waving, whooping, apparent madmen over the brow of the hill, racing down toward us. As we drove once again through the narrow gap in the trench, we saw the men putting the stones back, and taking a defensive position.

The chief waved and said, "Take the Bwana and the Totos and leave here quickly. This is dangerous. This is war."

We drove the short distance back into Nakasongola. We were both speechless. I felt a cold, clammy sensation, and the anger and adrenaline were beginning to die down sufficiently for me to feel frightened indeed. I glanced through the rear mirror as we drew out of sight of the group and saw the unmistakable signs of a clash between them.

As we pulled into the town, crowds of people gathered around us, particularly the two little Indians whom I had almost run over.

"Did you not see us? Did you not hear us? We were warning you. Did you not know there was danger down the road? We tried to stop you, sir."

I apologized and thanked them, and tried very briefly to explain what we'd encountered. We were encouraged immediately to drive to the police station where we could report these findings. When we arrived at the small police station, it was already surrounded by a varied crowd of people, black, white and brown, all demanding to know from the police what was going on. The poor policeman looked distraught and stood on the steps of the police station waving to ask them to be calm.

"All we know," he shouted, "is that the telephones have

been cut, and that we are out of communication with Kampala, and we do not know what's happening. My advice to all of you is that you go north back up the road that you've traveled, and do not attempt to go south into Kampala. It will be impossible and dangerous."

Angela squeezed my arm and pulled me away from the crowd. "He's right, you know. There's something very serious going on here. This is not just a bunch of robbers; this is an organized situation, and is a war. The farther from this place we get the better I'll like it," she said.

I'd begun to respect her feelings and her instinct. She was certainly someone who did not react emotionally and flippantly.

"After all, we have the lives of these little children to consider."

I nodded my assent. I searched through my pockets and found that I had some reserve Uganda shilling notes in the back of my wallet for an emergency. I never expected that particular variety of emergency.

"We've enough to fill up with petrol and get us back up to Massindi. It's about a three-hour drive; we'll get there after dark, but there's a hotel there and I'm sure they'll put us up."

As we were driving north again, retracing our steps up the red dusty road, I glanced frequently across at this young lady whom I had known for barely a day. She was introduced to me that morning at the hospital in Gulu, where I'd been visiting in my capacity as lecturer in pathology at the medical school in Kampala. One of my duties was to visit up-country hospital laboratories. The hospital superintendent asked if I would kindly take her and two small African children that she was escorting to a family in Kampala. She was only slightly shorter than I, somewhere in the region of five foot three or four, with light brown hair that had red and auburn streaks through it, and hung down onto her shoulders. Her nose had a slight upturned shape to it, and her smile was both open and generous. Her most striking feature, however, was the deep green of her eyes. She was one of those individuals who is easy to meet and easy to get on with. She was, she explained to me, a social worker, and had been doing some project in the up-country hospitals, and had been asked to take these children back to Kampala, but had no transportation at the time. I was delighted from the beginning. It wasn't very often that I traveled in East Africa in the presence of a beautiful young women who was so interesting and made me feel so relaxed.

As we drove north again, my thoughts went over and over those few short, but horribly vivid, moments that had just passed. How decisive she had been: no panic but a sense of organization and control. I reluctantly admitted to myself that she had taken the initiative. My old self-assurance, however, came back, and my hurt male pride was comforted to some extent by the smile and the way in which she leaned her head against my shoulder and murmured her thanks for saving their lives.

We drove for over an hour before either of us spoke about the events.

She suddenly lifted her head up from where she'd been leaning against the door, and quietly said, "You know, this situation is probably much more serious than we think."

I still could not bring myself to picture anything that serious going on in Uganda. I'd lived in the country for a year and a half, traveled widely, and never had any problems.

75

Everyone had always been friendly and happy. Granted, the political situation was not entirely desirable, and the rise to power of the Ugandan army under General Amin was a somewhat depressing prospect, but at that time the prime minister, Milton Obote, seemed to have everything under control, including his belligerent general. I tried to suppress thoughts of the uprisings in the Congo that were still in most people's minds at that time in East Africa. Although it was 1967, it had been only a few years before that horrors and bloodshed beyond description had taken place in the neighboring country.

My only immediate concern was that we would find a room at the hotel and that the proprietor would accept a check. This turned out to be no problem at all. In fact, the manager of the hotel was relieved to see us, having already heard from some other travelers of the seriousness of the situation. He began to try to apprise us of what was going on.

"All I've heard, Dr. Jones, is that other roads into Kampala apparently have been blocked. We've been trying to hear something on the radio, but no news is coming through, and all the telephones are nonfunctioning. Something bad's going on, that much we know. Anyway, don't you worry. The young lady and the two children are safely in their room, and you have a room, and don't worry about your check, it will be taken care of, I'm sure. Come and have a drink. It looks like you could do with one."

I must admit, I really did enjoy that gin and tonic as we sat on the verandah smoking our pipes.

Shortly after, Angela reappeared looking fresh from her bath, and prettier than ever. We were joined by a short, stocky man with a huge handlebar moustache, who spoke with a clipped European accent that matched his admitted origins as being a Swiss from Geneva. Pierre Duvale was a representative of the World Health Organization. He had been driving along one of the other main roads from the west and reached a similar roadblock, and took off in his small Peugeot car through the bush, through tracks, through side roads that certainly one would not find on the map, and finally made it to the road leading into Massindi. He looked like one of those tough, resourceful pioneer types who can make his way through all sorts of improbable difficulties, and certainly his history bore that out. He had worked with the WHO for years, and on one occasion had narrowly escaped death in Somalia, when he discovered that the Somali warlords there, and their politician friends, were using the WHO Land Rovers to ferry prostitutes from the brothel to their houses. He'd crept out that night, taken the distributor heads off all the Land Rovers, and the keys, put them in a parcel, sent them to Geneva and escaped.

"I've seen enough of Africa to know that this is big trouble," he said determinedly. "I'm heading up-country until this blows over. Nowhere that can be reached by road from Kampala will be safe. The next thing that will happen will be for that great ape, Idi Amin, to appear with the Ugandan army."

"But surely we could go to the police station here in Massindi and find out what they know," Angela said.

"Ahhh. A waste of time, my young friend," Duvale said. "These African police won't know anything. In any case, they're probably too scared to deal with it."

At that moment, a very strange trio arrived, three Italians who were employees of the Alitalia Airlines. They had been elephant hunting somewhere in the northeast. The spokesman of the group was well over six feet tall, with red hair, and built like an ox, and therefore somewhat incongruously speaking English with an Italian accent. The other two were small and dark; one of them could easily by his demeanor and his attitude have passed as a member of the Mafia. The third, a miserable whiny little man, kept moaning to himself in fear.

Having heard our story, the tall red-haired man announced defiantly, "We'll shoot our way through, eh?"

"Yes, we shoot our way through," the Mafia-like man agreed.

The third one whined even more.

"I don't think you understand," Richard said. "There are hundreds of them, armed to the teeth."

Duvale interrupted, saying, "They've already dealt with the police force who are armed with submachine guns on the other road, so don't be so stupid. You wouldn't even be able to load your elephant gun fast enough to save your life."

"Oh. Mama, mama!" whined the little Italian. "Let's stay here where it is safe."

They were interrupted by the hotel manager's assistant, who came out onto the verandah. "There's news on the radio from the BBC's overseas service. Quickly!"

They all rushed to the manager's small sitting room and listened intently as a bland BBC voice announced that there was fighting in the streets of Kampala, and clouds of black smoke billowed over the city. Without any sounds of emotion or disturbance in his voice, he calmly concluded that there was a bloodbath proceeding, and then continued with the latest cricket scores. They all sat in shocked silence. A few minutes later they managed to tune into the somewhat garbled account that came over from the local radio station, announcing that the Buganda tribe, led by Sir Edward Mutessa, had tried to overthrow the government. The prime minister, Milton Obote, and his chief of staff, Brigadier General Idi Amin, had called in the various units of the Ugandan army, and fighting was taking place in Kampala and in the surrounding countryside.

People thrown together in times of danger create a rapidly developing camaraderie, and we were no exception. That night we sat together in the dining room of the hotel, the Italians, the Swiss, Angela and myself, and despite the undercurrent of anxiety, the food and the wine, along with a bottle of brandy provided by the manager after dinner, helped our moods considerably. In fact, I was beginning to feel that perhaps this was much less serious than we thought, and it would blow over soon, and suggested that after all we'd be safe there in the hotel.

"Don't be too sure, my young friend," Duvale said. "You don't remember the Congo. I do. I was there. And a lot of innocent people were killed."

Why is that there is always someone in any company who will bring you back down to earth, and sometimes even below?

I was about to get angry with him, but Angela said, "I agree with you, monsieur. There is something else you may have overlooked, and that is -- how do we get back to Kampala? Or indeed, do we go back to Kampala? Or do we try an escape from the country if it becomes the situation that Mr. Duvale here seems to think it might?"

Duvale stood up and smoothed his moustache. "You

79

have three choices as I see it. You go west into the Congo, but that is like jumping out of the frying pan into the fire; or you go north to the Sudan, where there is already a tribal war raging; or you take the long northeastern route across Uganda to the border with Kenya."

"And what do you suggest?" I asked.

"Me?" said the Swiss, playing again with his moustache, "I intend to disappear into the bush until all this has calmed down. But if I were you with those children, I'd get the hell out of here to Kenya as quickly as possible. Keep to the side roads as long as you can, and avoid towns unless you need petrol, and cross the border north where there is no likelihood of interception."

Angela sat quietly, taking in all the information.

The red-haired manager of Alitalia suddenly announced in his loud voice, "I think we should all stay together. You know, safety in numbers. And, my friends and I have guns. We can at least protect you."

Duvale smiled at the Italian and said, "Thank you, senor, but numbers are a disadvantage in these times. I prefer to run alone. Also, you would add visibly to these young people and their charges. So, please go to Kenya by a different route."

The husky man shrugged his shoulders and spoke to his compatriots in Italian. They all said good night, and Duvale made his farewell.

Angela and I sat on the verandah alone beneath the clear starry sky.

"It's so beautiful," she murmured. "It's so difficult to imagine people are killing each other not far from here." With that she gently squeezed my hand.

I don't know how long we sat there just hand in hand, staring at the stars. Once again, as she did in the car, she leaned her head on my shoulder. I was afraid to say anything in case the spell would be broken. After all, last night we hadn't even met. I put my arm around her, and she snuggled closely.

"Don't worry. I promised to get you and those kids safely to Kampala. I didn't account for these kinds of difficulties, but by one means or another I promise I'll get you there. We'll be okay."

She murmured something inaudibly and turned her face up and kissed me gently on the lips.

The following morning, fate, nature and Africa conspired against me. I had one of my biannual attacks of dysentery. Some people can survive in Africa for years without having even a slight illness. Some of us are made of lesser stuff. Losing fluid from both ends of the body in a tropical climate is devastating, and I soon became a helpless mess lying on the bed, rapidly dehydrating. Angela ministered to me like an angel for that day and most of the following day, and finally managed to get a doctor from the local government hospital.

"Boy, you look in bad shape," he said professionally from the foot of the bed. "Better get you some fluids and some Enterovioform soon."

I tried to smile, but found even that an effort.

Angela asked him, "Do you know anything about the situation in Kampala?"

He said there was no news at all.

Eventually replacement fluids and some antibiotics brought the bout under control, and I began to keep down some fluids, and rapidly recovered. These few days did not,

81

in fact, put a blanket on our rapidly developing romantic situation. In fact, if anything, it brought us even closer together. If you can survive several days with someone with severe dysentery, and still feel a sense of tenderness and warmth toward them, that is rapidly approaching a situation of true love.

During those semi-delirious hours, my thoughts had repeatedly returned to the fate of my friends and comrades in Kampala. What was happening at the medical school? What was happening in the department of pathology? The professor and my dear friends -- were they safe? What had happened? It was very frustrating. There was still no news on the radio from England, still no news from Kampala, except that one traveler had rumored that Idi Amin had taken over power and that there were reprisals.

We decided that, weak though I was, we should delay no longer, and borrowing some money from the hotel manager and filling up the car with petrol, we decided to set off through some of the back roads toward the Kenyan border. Once we were safely out of Uganda, we could reassess the situation, not only from our own point of view, but the danger to the children. After all, these two small children, as Angela pointed out, were part of a high-class Buganda family, and these were the ones who had presumably caused the revolution, or whatever it was, and were certainly deadly enemies of Idi Amin and the government. For that reason alone, we had to escape. We had to get safely to an embassy.

By then I was quite familiar with most of the roads in Uganda, having traveled extensively in my research as a pathologist, and in my duties as lab inspector, but the roads we traveled on that day I doubt if anyone in a modern vehicle would have even been aware of. There were times when the car bounced over tree stumps and narrowly avoided going crashing through mud huts, and through the back of somebody's banana plantation. We nearly ran over chickens and goats, and under normal circumstances it might have been exciting or fun, but it was terrifying then. As we were driving through an area of heavy undergrowth, I happened to glance down and a red light was shining ominously on the dashboard.

Angela had already noticed it, and smiled and said, "Looks like your dynamo is gone."

I thought rapidly. As long as we kept moving and didn't stop the car and try to start it again, and as long as we didn't need to travel at night and use lights, we could probably survive until we got to the next town. The question was -- how long would that take? And would someone in such a town be able to fix it?

We quietly drove into the tiny town of Lyra. It consisted of one street with some small Indian shops, a bank, and a small police station at one end of the town. Very prominently displayed, however, was 'Mr. R. Singh, Car Mechanic.' My heart lifted. If anyone could fix it, he could. Those Sikhs in East Africa could probably repair a Rolls Royce.

We drove up, and the turbaned, bearded, huge man greeted us warmly, inspected the car and announced that the "dynamo was finished."

I was about to sheepishly ask if there was any possible way it could be repaired when he said, "But do not fear, my friends. I have such a dynamo on my shelf. Ford Consul, Mark III -- yes."

Angela and I looked at each other in utter amazement.

83

"Can you imagine," she said, "anywhere in Britain, or America, arriving in a town this size and somebody being able to put on what sounds like a new or reconditioned dynamo off the shelf?"

"You know, Africa will never cease to surprise me," I said.

We were instructed to go down the road into a small shop that was run by his sister, where we were given tea, while he put the new dynamo in the car. The embarrassing moment came when payment was required.

"Mr. Singh, I realize this is somewhat unusual, but we are in some difficult circumstances, and...would you please accept a check?"

"Of course, sir. You are a doctor; you are an Englishman. That is good enough for me."

I was about to say, Actually I'm a Welshman, but the point had been made.

We drove on down the road, and by now the sun was beginning to set. It was too late to continue the journey to the next major town of Mbale, and far too late to reach the safety of the Kenyan border. If we tried to cross it by one of the more unusual spots it would be extremely dangerous at night. I began to feel desperate. What were we to do? And then for the first time in many years, I began to pray.

I don't know why, or how, God hears or answers our prayers at times, and He hadn't heard from me for quite some time, but suddenly a notice at the side of the road, pointing left down a dirt track, announced 'Kumi Leprosarium.' In my more innocent, and perhaps better, days as a medical student, I had belonged to the Medical Missionary Association, and was prepared to be sent anywhere in the world to heal the sick and preach the gospel. The couple in charge of our welfare had been doctor and nurse of Kumi Leprosarium -- Uganda. We had been told about that place so many times that the name was forever imprinted in my mind, and there, suddenly, it was. Without hesitating I made a sharp left turn and we started down the road.

Angela looked up in horror. "Where on earth are we going? Didn't it say Leprasorium? You're not taking me to a leper colony, for goodness sake, are you?"

"Don't worry, please," I said. "You know, this disease is not as contagious as it sounds. It's not the Black Death, and we're not living in the Middle Ages. You wouldn't believe how coincidental, if you want to call it that, this is." Then briefly I told her the story.

She squeezed my arm and looked at me with such positive reassurance. "Then it must be so," she said.

When we arrived at the collection of buildings, we were greeted by a tall, thin man in baggy khaki shorts. His wife took Angela and the two children so they could wash and be comfortable, and put the children to bed. Dr. Phillips and I sat down on the porch outside of his house, and I told him the whole story. He looked grim and sat silently listening to every word.

"Well..." he said and he reached out and touched me on the shoulder, "you needn't worry. You're safe here. This is probably the safest place on earth. You know how superstitious our African friends are about lepers. Believe me, no one will come here."

I felt that he was right. Then I told him, reluctantly, about my days in the Medical Missionary Association.

"Oh! Old Dr. Bennett! Yes. Yes, I remember him well.

Wonderful man. Well, so you didn't come to Africa as a missionary, but you still came, didn't you?" he said, as if he understood my inner thoughts and that which had plagued me for some time.

Phillips was the sort of man to whom you could pour out your soul because his sincerity was so obvious. A man who lives out there in the middle of patients with leprosy, away from even the civilized centers of Africa, is not one whose faith is based on some superficial or trivial event. Talking to him was cathartic indeed, and I felt much better by the time we all sat down to dinner. When we started with a prayer of thanks for our delivery I could barely stem the tears. It had been so long.

After dinner, Dr. Phillips asked me if I would assist him with the weekly film show for the patients. The ladies busied themselves in some fashion while Phillips and I went to an open field that was used for all sorts of activities in the daytime, and served as a kind of open-air cinema at night. The screen was placed, and the projector, and then sitting on the grass under the stars, surrounded by lepers, I saw a film about Tunbridge Wells. The green fields and hedgerows of old England were in such contrast to the situation in which I found myself. The almost overwhelming homesickness was partially put into perspective, and my thoughts returned to that beautiful green-eyed girl whom I would never otherwise have met had it not been for the events of that day. Certainly, if our journey back to Kampala had been the normal, relatively uneventful, one, we would not now be in love.

Two days later, with warm handshakes, hugs and kisses, and the promise of prayers on our behalf, we said farewell to the Phillips and set off on the continuation of the road to

Kenya. It was remarkably uneventful. There were no road barriers, there were no signs of disturbance, the place looked exactly as it had always looked, and no one seemed to be in any way concerned.

It was almost like an anticlimax, until we came to the rock at Tororo. This was a famous landmark, and a hotel stood on the left side of the road, and in front the border with Kenya, which in those days had no frontier post. The only indication that you had left Uganda was the sudden deterioration of the road, which went from tarmac to dirt.

I was about to suggest that we stop for a cup of coffee at the hotel, as I had always done when I traveled on that road, when the urgency came back to me. A look from Angela clearly indicated we should continue while we had the chance. Unfortunately, that chance abruptly ended. There was, indeed, a road barrier. There were army trucks and police vehicles blocking the only way out of the country.

The police officer was extremely polite, and simply indicated that no one was allowed to leave the country. All was well in Kampala, but for various reasons we would be escorted back there safely. It was pretty clear that we had no choice, and the armed soldiers who stood in the background reinforced the determination that the quiet voice of the policeman represented. We were allowed, however, to have that desperately needed cup of coffee at the hotel, and as we walked dejectedly into the dining room we were greeted by a sea of familiar faces. There were the three Italians, and a couple of others whom we had seen in Massindi Hotel, and there, playing furiously with his moustache, was Pierre Duvale.

They greeted us warmly, and we sat and exchanged

stories.

"It seems, my friend," Duvale said, "that we are to be escorted back into Kampala, which means we are now prisoners, you understand."

"Oh, for goodness sake!" the red-haired Italian said, "I see no danger. I think they are merely doing this for political reasons, you understand."

Duvale sat down. He obviously enjoyed the dramatic sides of life and was hardly the epitome of optimism.

That last stretch of the road back to Kampala was a strange experience. I'd driven it many times before on medical safaris, and on fishing trips, but never before had I been in an armed convoy. At the front was a truck with a machine gun mounted on the top, and then all of our cars in line, ours being the last. Behind us was another truck, also mounted with a machine gun.

I expected the journey to be slow and ponderous, but it was exactly the opposite. It was terrifying. We drove at the pace of the leading vehicle, about as fast as my old Ford would go, and since we were only a few feet apart from each other it was like being on the Los Angeles freeway. Every so often the convoy would suddenly come to a grinding halt that would make the sweat stand out on my brow, and Angela would cling very close to me, not that I objected to that.

There was one particular occasion when we stopped in the bottom of a valley. The side of the road, on both sides, was covered with trees, the only forested area along the entire route.

I turned to Angela. "I hate to be like Duvale, but this has got to be the worst place where one could stop. If anybody wanted to ambush us, this is where they would choose."

The soldiers got out of the truck behind us, stretched, and walked across the road where a poor, dejected old man in rags was sitting with a pile of charcoal on a small stand. They proceeded to beat him with their rifles until he ran off into the bush screaming, and stole his charcoal.

"So much for the Ugandan army," I said. "Not only that, but if ever there was likely now to be a retaliation..."

Angela looked at me and smiled. "You're beginning to sound more and more like Pierre Duvale every moment."

The rest of the journey was remarkably uneventful. Finally we entered the familiar streets of Kampala and were deposited in the center of the town where both the police and the soldiers melted away. It was a tremendous anticlimax.

We all got out of our cars, looked at each other in amazement, decided it was time to shake hands and say good-bye, hugged each other, kissed each other, and went our separate ways. I took Angela to the home of the two small children, where she would be staying overnight, and with a gentle good night kiss, since that was all that was allowed us, we vowed to meet again the following day.

I then decided I'd better make my way to the professor's house, and let him know that I was back safely, and indeed, to see if all my comrades were safe. I found a group of them sitting on the lawn, since it was late afternoon, drinking tea. It looked like an English garden party. When the professor saw me, he left his guests, ran across the lawn, and seized hold of me in a warm hug, like a father would greet a son.

"Well, you little prodigal. So you've returned to us," he said, beaming. "You know, they told us that you'd been killed. The British High Commission actually sent a notice to England saying 'Missing, believed dead.'"

"Well, it was close, prof," I said.

"Ahh, come and join the others," he said. "Come and let's celebrate your safe arrival."

The tea was rapidly changed for more suitable libations, and then, to my chagrin, Cameron and MacDonald began to vie with each other for the telling of their tales of woe.

"Oh, you should have seen it, Richard!" MacDonald exclaimed. "Ugandan army comes tearing up the road from Jinja after the Kabakas people tried to block all the roads -- well, of course you know about that."

I just remained silent.

"And then there was a hell of a battle going on. They started to shell the Kabakas' palace, you know, on the hill over there. Well, you can imagine it. There was Professor Simmons from London trying to give a lecture, with mortars coming over the top of the medical school. Wow! Talk about stiff upper lip. He held that class together despite the occasional blasts that shook the building."

"But then," Cameron interjected, "what about when they finally made that bayonet charge up the hill, found the gates of the Kabakas palace enclosure wide open, and go charging straight in? There were those old veterans of the King's East African Rifles with machine guns, and they mowed 'em down like grass."

I sat back with a sigh. It began to make my experience less and less dramatic.

"Well, then they got mad as hell," MacDonald took over the story again. "So they started shelling the place, and did some pretty nasty damage. Then they made a mass charge up the hill. And what happened? It starts to rain. So you know what the glorious Ugandan army does? They stand under the trees until the rain stops. Meanwhile, the Kabaka nips over the back wall of the palace, and is secreted away by his fanatical followers, and apparently took a canoe across Lake Victoria to the Sesse Island, and is probably by now in England in the Strand Palace Hotel."

Everyone started to laugh.

I sat back, wondering what sort of response to make. "Well, I'm glad you're all alive and well," I said.

"Ah, well, this damned curfew that we've got, though, at seven every evening, and those blasted apes of Idi Amin's wandering the streets is no joke. You'll find life's changed a lot in this short period of time," Cameron said to me.

"Well, Richard, tell us about your adventures," the prof said.

"Ah, well, after what you people have gone through it's pretty tame, really, a bit of a problem on the road. You know that stretch of road by Nakasongola? Just one of those things, you understand." And they continued with their animated discussion and descriptions of the aborted revolution, with Buganda against the rest of Uganda.

I vowed that one day I would tell my story, and recall those violent days in Uganda, but time has mellowed me, and some of the audience by now will have subsequently died, or have been scattered across the world. What I do remember most about that short stretch of red dusty road on that early Uganda evening is not the screaming savages, the spears thrown, or the passive serious look of the men who pulled the stones away, it is the look of fierce and protective determination in those deep green eyes that even now stare at me across the room.

Guarding the group

THREE MEN

IN A BOAT

ON THE NILE

A large crowd of excited Africans, men, women and children, gathered around what to them must have seemed a strange sight indeed. The three white men were standing, staring down into a rubber dinghy, that had a small outboard motor attached to the rear. "It's a hell of a lot smaller than I thought it would be, Allen," Richard exclaimed.

Allen returned to his companion, and with a smile simply said, "Oh, it's big enough. "After all, we're three Welshmen, not the biggest people in the world." He laughed loudly. The third man simply sat wringing his hands and mumbling something in Welsh, only partly audibly.

"Well, now we've come this far, I suppose we'd better get on with it," Richard said reluctantly. With no more

93

hesitation, Allen Reese stepped into the back of the boat and took command of the tiller. He pointed for Richard to go into the prow, and between the two of them they partly dragged and partly cajoled their poor little companion, who reverted entirely to the Welsh language.

Richard nervously positioned himself in the prow of the boat and with the other two seated, the boat pushed off from the shore to the cheers and adulation of the crowd. Reese responded with all of his nature, waving, cheering, and singing. Richard smiled to himself and thought, What an idiot I am. Why am I sitting here in a small rubber dinghy with a madman and someone who is liable to throw himself out of the boat in anxiety? And all to go fishing.

The three young men had one thing in common; they all worked for the University of East Africa in different capacities, and they were all from the small country of Wales. There the resemblance ended.

Allen Reese, the steersman and driver of the boat, was the tallest of the three, being somewhat below five-foot-eight, very athletic in proportion, and bronzed with many hours luxuriously enjoying the sunshine. He was known to be a great socializer, and his job at the university was not particularly demanding. In fact, if you wanted to see Allen Reese from three-thirty on any particular day, he would probably be found on the tennis court. He was a handsome fellow, and seemed to have no trouble in charming everyone, including his friend Richard, who was sitting at the front end of the boat wondering how he had ever gotten involved with this man Reese in the first place.

Richard was second tallest of the trio, being five-foot-six-and-a-half, as he always proudly announced. He had the same dark hair and dark eyes, but his skin was quite pale. He had not been exposed to the sun as had his colleague Reese. Richard was a hardworking young pathologist at the medical school, and this was one of the rare occasions when he went out, except on medical safaris. Not to say he was a serious and morose character, far from it. Richard certainly enjoyed many aspects of life. He particularly loved fishing, and of all fishing the pursuit of the Nile perch on this upper stretch of the White Nile in Uganda.

The third man in the boat, whose name was Hayden Jones (there is a sad shortage of surnames in Wales), was one of the most nervous men Richard had ever encountered. He was the shortest of them, and appeared to be in a constant state of anxiety. He also stuttered furiously. As a result he rarely spoke unless asked fairly strong questions requiring immediate answers. So often his friends became irritated with him in waiting for answers that they avoided asking questions in the first place. Hayden and his wife were born in a small village in North Wales, one of those small enclaves of Welsh-speaking Welshness that very few people have discovered. In an international community such as the one in Kampala it was a great surprise to hear the two of them speaking in broken English to foreigners who assumed that they were British. They never spoke anything other than Welsh to each other, and had done that since they were children.

Why young Hayden Jones came with the two of them remained a mystery. He was never known to go anywhere without his wife, whereas Allen Reese, in complete contrast, rarely ever went anywhere with Pamela, unless he was forced to by some social occasion. Part of the problem was that

Reese in his cups would frequently and generously invite all sorts of varied guests to dinner at his home, and then completely forget about it, and what was more devastating, forget to tell his wife. There had been so many occasions when embarrassed guests had turned away from the door finding Reese not at home, and his wife with her hair in curlers. Richard's relationship with Rosemary was somewhere in between. She really preferred to stay at home, loved the garden, and one thing she did not enjoy was fishing. To be fair, however, as Richard reminded himself as he sat there in the boat, She doesn't object to me going. Reese had probably made all sorts of incredible tales about where he was actually going to be on that particular day, and why Mrs. Hayden Jones let her passive husband out of her sight he couldn't fathom at all.

Richard enjoyed the surroundings. This was not his first experience of the Nile, but previously it was in a large boat. He had never been that close to the water before.

The white-headed fish eagles plunged into the water and emerged with fish clasped in their talons. There was a strange mixture of smells consisting of fresh water, green vegetation and the smoke of charcoal fires from the bank.

The dinghy chugged along with the water occasionally spilling in. It made him realize what a powerful and potentially deadly river they were in. This was not the placid, broad, slowly moving Nile of Egypt but a rushing river strewn with rocks and islands, and unexpected small cataracts. The stretch they were on had no actual waterfalls, and so he was not worried. There were, however, some nasty pieces of jagged rock sticking out of the water at points throughout the river.

"This was a great idea to get this rubber dinghy, Richard," Allen boomed from the other end of the boat, smiling as usual.

Richard nodded, and admitted to himself, Well, it was my crazy idea, I suppose.

The fact of the matter was that Allen Reese was dying to go Nile perch fishing after he had heard Richard boasting about the huge fish that he'd caught. After all, a seventy-five pound Nile perch was a pretty formidable catch for a small Welshman whose largest catch was a pound and a half. But, as usual, Reese had run out of money and whatever allowance his wife gave him was certainly not enough to hire a boat with a driver and guides.

He prevailed upon Richard to approach the group from the Walter Reed Army Unit, stationed at the medical school. He had heard some rumor to the effect that they had an inflatable dinghy which they used on some trips. To Richard's amazement, the head of the Walter Reed Unit, who was a kindly man and quite friendly toward the members of the department, willingly allowed him to have the boat, the engine, and even provided fuel. This meant that all they had to do was muster enough money among them to drive to the small launching place on the Nile, some sixty miles from Kampala, and that would be their total expense.

The Walter Reed man had assured Richard that the boat was quite sturdy. It was good by American military standards, and it would take some pretty powerful rocks to puncture the thick rubber hull. It did look sturdy, and sitting in it, he felt reasonably secure. It was the closeness to the water that was the most startling.

"You know, Allen, the only thing that worries me is if we

97

hit one of those really big Nile perch, and it ran under the boat, you know, with its dorsal fin up...."

Reese interrupted him. "Oh, don't be so stupid. We'll maneuver the boat so the fish can't run under it," he exclaimed. This was typical of Reese. He lived life in a total state of abandon, without giving thought to any of the consequences.

There was still not even a murmur from Hayden Jones, who sat crunched up in the middle of the boat, afraid to move.

Richard was reminded by a favorite expression of his father's, "Boy, I'll be glad when I've had enough of this," and sat back and tried to enjoy the surrounding scenery once again.

The next few hours were dreamy and largely uneventful. They trailed the lure behind the boat, but nothing seemed to respond. At least two of the occupants of the small craft were grateful. And then, as so often happens in that part of East Africa, the clouds opened up and a torrential rain came down. Luckily, the dinghy was close to a small island in the middle of the river. They immediately headed for it and managed without capsizing to beach the craft, and brought it to the shore under the shelter of a tree.

In half an hour the rain had stopped, and once again they pushed out into the current and spent another hour of fruitless fishing.

Richard looked at his watch. "Heck, it's four already. Considering how far we've drifted downstream with the current, we'd better get back as soon as possible, or we'll have to drive home in the dark."

Reese reluctantly agreed, and they turned about with

some difficulty. They had not realized how strong that current was until they tried to work the small engine and the rather clumsy craft against it.

It was the first time since they'd been out all day that young Hayden Jones had played an active role. They allowed him to sit at the tiller, and at first they made slow progress upstream. They reached one of the areas where the current was stronger, having bounced around some rocky outlets in the path of the water. Suddenly the engine, pushed to its limit and screaming in protest, reverted to a stunned silence. Young Jones broke into an excited and unexpected performance that made him look like a hysterical ballet dancer. He leapt up and down, screaming at the motor in Welsh, and pulled furiously at the cord. Before either of the other two could stop him, he yanked at the cord with such fury that it snapped off, and he fell flat into the rocking boat.

One of Allen Reese's great qualities was that he rarely ever panicked. This was as good a time as any to panic, but he was one of those organized and disciplined men, underneath his laissez faire attitude. He leapt to the back of the boat with amazing agility, and proceeded to club the hysterical Jones into the bottom of the boat, shouting, "Get down there, you stupid bastard. I'll kill you, you rotten stinking North Walean. Get down there before I kick you in the river."

Hayden cowered on the floor of the dinghy as Reese took control. Richard seized hold of the two oars, and tried to use one of them to control their progress, which was now rapidly downstream once again. It did not take Reese long to realize that he could not reach the starting cord. It had snapped off inside the motor. He swore in English and his few words of

99

Welsh, and picking up the oar threatened to beat Jones. Richard intervened and pointed out that they were going downstream at an increasing speed, and on the opposite side of the river from where the car was parked.

Allen Reese snapped out of his fury and surveyed the scene. Seizing the other oar and pulling with all their might, he and Richard managed to turn the boat around. They flogged the water with the paddles until their muscles could barely move. The sweat was pouring off in streams when Richard saw a tree which seemed to be there ages before. Reese noted his glance and nodded in agreement.

"We're not making any progress at all. We're barely holding our own. This is not going to work." No longer panic-stricken or angry, he became very cold and calculating.

"I wish we could make it to the other bank and walk back to the car or get help, but that's too dangerous. We'd better make for the closest shore we can, which is right here." With that he guided the boat toward a small clearing in the papyrus groves. It was with a great sense of relief that Richard's feet found firm ground again, even though it was on the wrong side of the Nile and in a totally unknown spot with the dusk coming on.

No one in his right mind wandered around the African bush at night. He guessed that there must be another hour or so before it really got dark, but what were they going to do? Nevertheless, he felt a great sense of gratitude and relief that he wasn't being borne down the river to the next rapids, and goodness knows what else.

By the time they hauled the dinghy out, panting for breath and soaked in sweat, a small group of locals had gathered around to exchange the usual greetings in Swahili of "Jambo" and "Habari." Richard was not in the mood for conversation. His throat was parched and he was feeling less than pleased with life. Reese, however, spoke Swahili fluently, and immediately started a conversation. Richard had been in East Africa for approximately a year and a half, and felt that he was quite familiar with the strange outfit that some of the local Africans wore. This, however, was almost theatrical. The most prominent individual was a man in his late fifties, wearing ragged dirty shorts and an old but well preserved double-breasted black dinner jacket. He was the local chief. When he realized the boat was not functioning, he volunteered to send one of his boys upstream to get help from the Indian who rented the fishing boats.

At this point, Hayden Jones, who had remained silent and cowed, leapt to his feet. "I'll go, boys. It's all my fault. Ah, Diew, Diew, it's all my fault," he mumbled, reverting to Welsh again.

Reese just snapped, "Yes, you're bloody right, it's all your fault, you stupid sod. I think you're the one who ought to go." Richard was about to tell Reese to lay off, but the look in the latter's eyes stopped him.

Hayden, wanting to prove his penitence, stepped closer to Reese's arm and received a healthy clout around the ear. The Africans looked in amazement. Violence, particularly in front of others, was out of character. Within a few minutes, Jones was running with the chief's messenger. Richard wondered if they would ever see any of them again.

"There he goes," mumbled Reese, "like bloody 'Saunders of the river.' I suppose he thinks he's Tarzan now as well."

Richard just sat down and smiled. Reese poked about inside the boat, and then came out with their last bottle of beer. Richard's mouth almost cracked in anticipation at the sight of the precious nectar; warm though it might be, it was about to have a profound therapeutic effect on him. Reese hesitated and glanced around. The chief in the double-breasted dinner jacket was looking at the bottle with an even greater desire. There was a petite African woman sitting cross-legged on the ground also looking covetously up at Reese.

"Oh, hell," said Allen. "We'd better give it to him."

"What! Must we?" said Richard.

"Well, look at it this way, boy-o. We're at their mercy. It's getting dark, we need their help. Surely you understand."

Richard knew his friend was right. Reese handed the bottle over to the chief with great ceremony. A look of sheer delight came over the old man's face. The woman looked even more pleased, and she jumped up and down. The old man bowed elegantly, seriously, and exclaimed, "Asanti sana," Swahili for 'thank you.' Then the chief bit the metal cap off the bottle and to the horror of the two young men, poured the beer into the bush and gave the empty bottle to the woman, who clasped it to her bosom as if it were the most treasured possession she had ever received. She ran off into the bush, giggling and hooting like a small child.

Richard and Allen stared at the ground until finally they burst out laughing. The old chief, puzzled by their reaction, extended his hand.

"This is a crazy country, Allen," Richard said. "I don't think I'm ever going to get used to it."

Darkness came with the usual rapidity that characterizes nightfall close to the equator, and Richard admitted to feeling somewhat anxious.

Then they heard the sound of a motor coming down the river. Soon they could see search lights blinking across the water, and finally focusing on their chosen spot on the bank. A metal boat with a metal awning on the top and a light at the front, piloted by some Indians, finally came into the small bay.

They boarded the boat, the dinghy was towed behind them, and it took all the money they had among them, and some IOUs, to pay for the escapade. As they finally pulled away in the Land Rover, having collapsed the dinghy appropriately to be shoved into the back rather unceremoniously, Richard was about to say, "Well, this damned trip cost us more than it would if we'd hired a proper boat in the first place," but decided that there was no point.

The dangers were not yet quite over. As they came around the first bend in the road from the river, they found a vast expanse of water where the road had been. The storm that they had experienced had obviously been more severe up river. It was not possible to gauge the depth of the water in front of them, and the more experienced Reese pointed out to Richard that trying to drive through it would be extremely dangerous since there might be potholes deep enough to sink them for the rest of the night.

At that point, Hayden Jones, once again, came to life. "I'll go, boys. I'll walk in front of the car. It's all my fault, it's all my fault."

"Oh, don't bring that up again," said Reese, irritably. "Get out there and see us safely through or shut up."

With that, young Hayden Jones marched in front of the vehicle up to his waist like a dejected and miserable, yet penitent and almost grateful man. By the time they reached

Kampala it was now well into the night, and Richard was wondering about the reception they would receive from their respective spouses. The first house they reached was that of Hayden Jones. His diminutive wife ran down from the house, and grasped him in her arms. There was a great deal of weeping and crying, mostly in Welsh, as if he had returned from the dead.

Reese sat there shaking his head. "Look at those silly buggers. It won't be like that when I get home, you can bet your life." When they did reach Reese's bungalow, there was his petite woman armed with a large stick, standing ominously at the end of the drive.

Before Allen could utter a word, she shouted, "Reese, get your backside into this house before I break this stick over your head. I've already notified the police that you're probably dead; maybe I'll make sure of it." Allen shrugged his shoulders and with his characteristic smile bade Richard good night.

Richard started, as if to get out of the vehicle and explain what had happened, but she stopped him in his tracks. "Richard Jones, go home before I lay this stick over you as well."

When Richard got to his own bungalow, his houseboy, Sam, was sitting patiently smoking his pipe on the verandah.

"Oh, Bwana. Are you well?"

"Yes. Tell Mrs. Jones that I'm back, would you?"

"Yes." And with that he rushed into the house.

As Richard walked away from the Land Rover, trying to stretch himself from the ache in his back, Rosemary appeared at the doorstep.

"Good fishing?" she asked nonchalantly, as if he'd just

been down the road for an hour or so in a local pond.

"Ah, no," Richard sighed. "Not one of my better days." Smiling to himself he entered the house and fixed himself a large gin and tonic. "That," he said quietly to himself, "is the last time I go fishing with two Welshmen."

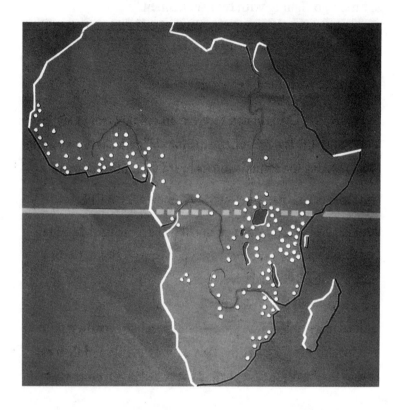

THE SHOESHINE BOY

OF ADDIS ABABA

"Those are very fine shoes, sir," the small boy said as he crouched over Richard's feet. The face that looked up at him had aquiline Hamitic features with a tall forehead so characteristic of Ethiopians. The large eyes and shining teeth seemed to fill his face with an innocence that was beguiling.

The boy continued to lovingly caress the shoes. "They are truly lovely, sir, but are in need of my expert cleaning." Richard smiled. "Yes, they are my favorite shoes," he said, wondering why he had answered the child. He had no intentions of subjecting himself to the attentions of a shoeshine boy in the streets of Addis Ababa. However, the shoes were in need of cleaning, and they were rather special.

"Please, sir, both your beautiful shoes and myself would be better if you let me clean them. I will do a wonderful job. I am an expert," the boy said. The look of joy had turned into an equally convincing one of deep sorrow. Richard could not walk away.

He had been in the capital of Ethiopia barely twenty-four

hours and had already been accosted by more beggars and would-be salesmen than during his previous two months in Zimbabwe. Yet, somehow this boy was different. Richard sat down at the edge of a low wall in the sparse garden which occupied the center of the main street outside the Hilton International Hotel. It was like a small oasis of trees and shrubs with some seating and a walled enclosure forming a barrier between the two lanes of the main highway that extended from the hotel to the city center.

The boy did not squander the opportunity. His face once more took on a look of optimism. He produced a small carrying box filled with the tools of his trade and rapidly began the process of cleaning the shoes. Richard watched him idly and thought of the past twenty-four hours.

There was confusion and chaos at the airport and the lack of friendliness in the entire process of entering the country of Ethiopia. It was such a contrast from his other experiences in Africa. What have I done to deserve this? he thought. He was told that the ruling communist regime did not like Americans, but he still had a British accent and at that time still carried a British passport even though it did say his domicile was the USA. Perhaps that was the problem.

The taxi from the airport to the hotel was a large yellow Mercedes Benz. It slowly meandered through the crowded streets lined by pedestrians and on several occasions barely avoided collisions with the numerous mule trains which seemed to be the other standard form of transportation. He had never seen anything quite like this before -- raggedly dressed, dejected-looking men with long whips driving the long lines of up to ten mules, laden with bundles of wood and charcoal. He was familiar with the blend of ancient and modern in Africa, but this was unique.

As they entered the outskirts of Addis Ababa, the car passed under a gigantic arch with a huge sign which stated (in English), Proletariate of the World Unite. It almost made him laugh, but the grimness of the surroundings and the lackluster look in the faces of passersby made him sad. The capital of Ethiopia had buildings which showed the Western influence, but as if to reinforce the obvious political influence, in the main square of the city, there stood a larger than life statue of Lenin shaking his fist into the air. Even the relatively gentle country of Zimbabwe had claims to socialism and called themselves comrades, but it was nothing like this.

All the African cities Richard had visited during the years were crowded with a variety of ancient vehicles, people, bicycles, goats and all of the paraphernalia of life. Addis was no exception. It was not the mule trains intersecting with Mercedes taxis and the obvious signs of powerful political affiliations that impressed Richard the most. It was the look of sadness and despair in the eyes of the people. The exuberant laughter and shouting of other African cities seemed to be missing. He was reminded of a description of life in Bulgaria.

The ultimate in contrast awaited him at the hotel. It was the largest Hilton he had ever seen. There was a long driveway from the dirty main road up to the entrance to the hotel and even in the course of that short journey he counted at least three huge swimming pools on the grounds. There was an air of wealth rarely encountered in Africa. It reminded him of the most exclusive country clubs in America.

The Mirage was broken by the sight of the worst shanty town of tin-roofed houses he had ever seen, actually leaning on the fence of the hotel a few yards away from one of its main swimming pools.

Richard felt glad that he was only staying until his flight to Cairo the following morning. He really had not planned to be in Addis in the first place and it was only because of airline schedules that he was there at all. He persuaded himself that he really did not belong among the clientele that he saw wandering quite unconcernedly through the grounds and the corridors of the hotel.

Normally, Richard enjoyed visiting new cities and usually took the opportunity to walk extensively. He was warned not to leave the hotel under any circumstances and, for once, took the advice to heart.

His recent bout of dysentery even prevented him from enjoying the wonderful Ethiopian food offered in the restaurant. He was glad indeed, when the following morning came. There was only an hour to wait for the bus to the airport. He decided to risk strolling out through the front entrance of the hotel into the modest collection of trees in the center of the road.

As he drifted out of his reverie he noticed that the shoeshine boy was applying all sorts of materials from tiny tins and pots to his shoes. Oh, God, I hope he'll be safe, Richard thought. These shoes were indeed special, a reminder of his days of hardship and struggle.

Richard remembered the day in Washington, D.C. when his three children persuaded him to buy those fine Italian leather shoes. They were on sale in a fancy shop that did not sell footwear. The mannequin that wore them was being dismantled and the shoes were available. Little did they realize that he had spent his last fifty dollars pleasing them. They seemed so genuinely concerned. The shoes he was wearing at the time were so cheap and worn. It was the last day he would spend with the children for quite some time. They had to return to their mother's home and he to Africa. They wanted him to have those display shoes in the store window. It was the pocket money he had intended sharing between them before he said good-bye and somehow they sensed it, and were even more persistent as if to tell him it was their gift to him. He realized that they loved him despite everything.

He looked down and inspected the final touches of the shoeshine operation. His eyes lit up. The shoes looked as good as the day he bought them. They were handmade of light, almost yellow leather with horizontal stitches across the front and layers of leather forming a short compound heel. He rarely wore them except on special occasions and thought how strange it was that he had them on that day. After all, he was about to take the bus to the airport and had really no need to wear them.

Until that moment Richard was longing to leave the depressed city and looked forward to the decadent, but colorful and lively, Cairo. The young boy, whom Richard estimated to be about eleven or twelve years old, was buffing and polishing yet again and murmuring with delight. "Did I not tell you, sir, how wonderful I would make these shoes?" "You did, indeed, my friend. They have never looked better," Richard said warmly. "Tell me, is this your chosen profession?" "Oh, no, no, sir, definitely not! I am studying at school and this job is to provide my books and pens. One day

111

I want to be an airline pilot."

Richard suppressed a smile. He sadly thought how unlikely such an event would ever take place. "I hope your dream comes true. Here is something that I hope will help." And he handed the boy a US fifty-dollar note that was kept for emergencies in the back of his wallet.

As the airport bus pulled out of the hotel driveway, Richard saw the shoeshine boy running from across the street waving and cheering and running alongside the belching black-smoked bus, which he followed for several hundred yards almost to the center of town. Richard leaned out of the window. "Be a good student and the best airline pilot in the world," he shouted. As the boy disappeared into the crowd, Richard sat back and sighed. "I hope he makes it," he said quietly. He mused about the fifty-dollar bill. "That's what I paid for the shoes," he said, remembering.

As the plane gained altitude Richard hoped he would never have to return to Addis again.

PART 2

"What are you doing in Ethiopia? And in this particular area?" The tall, gaunt-looking man in a disheveled, stained military uniform spoke with a hard cruelty, and his eyes were penetrating.

"I keep telling you, but you don't seem to want to believe me. I'm working for the WHO and my plane crashed in those hills over there and I managed to get to this village." Richard was sitting in an old wicker chair trying to lean his back against the table, staring up at the tall man and his two heavily armed assistants who guarded the door. His left arm ached intolerably. He was worried that it might be broken. His clothes were torn in several places and he was barefoot.

"You have no papers. No identity. No baggage. Why should I believe you?," the tall man answered coldly. "I was robbed on my way from the crash to the village. The bastards even took my watch and my shoes!," Richard said. At this point he almost felt like crying and had to abruptly stop himself as he saw the look of disdain in his captors' eyes. "Look, I have nothing to do with your civil war. I just want to get out of the way and back to my family." Richard was stopped by a hard slap across his face. "Silence! You come here to my country on some pretense and when things get rough you think you can pack up and leave. You will regret coming to Ethiopia! We will find out who sent you!"

The man turned on his heel and left the room and Richard leaned back on the rickety old chair breathing heavily. He felt a horrible sense of desperation that seemed to permeate his whole being. Palpitations migrated to his stomach with nausea that was almost uncontrollable. Why would they not believe him, he was telling the truth! It wasn't his fault that the damned plane en route to Eritria was forced to land in the rebel-held south of Ethiopia.

Richard's thoughts returned to the last time he visited this country nearly fifteen years earlier. He remembered it being pretty depressing then; except, for that one...His thoughts were interrupted by the sound of gunfire all around the building and before he could respond the door burst open and two men in khaki uniforms seized him by each arm. He shrieked in pain as he was dragged outside. It was dark. He suddenly realized how long his stay in that room had been. It

113

was early in the morning when he had staggered into the village and was captured. He felt certain that he was going to die, and started praying under his breath for courage and for his family.

Then he saw the plane. It was a four-engine antique from the Second World War, a sort of nondescript grey-green in color with khaki coloring to the wings. To his amazement he was bundled into the dark interior and slumped on a bench on one side of the fuselage. The men sat on either side of him. As the plane began to taxi along the roadway (he remembered seeing no airstrip earlier in the day), his anxiety returned with a vengeance.

"Surely you're not going to take off with no runway," Richard said. One of the men beamed a smile at him from the semidarkness. "Do not worry. The pilot is the best. He can get us out of here." The man's confidence was infectious and Richard sat back as the plane made increasingly agonizing sounds as it shuddered along the ground. There was a feeling of an upward movement and he was barely prevented from falling to the back of the plane. They were actually flying. He was glad there were no windows and it was dark. Whoever the pilot is, he thought, he sure knows how to fly this old crate. His composure gradually returned even though his pulse was still racing. "Where are you taking me? And by the way, who are you?" The man to his left smiled and replied, "We are members of the Liberation Army of the People of Ethiopia and we take you to safety."

Richard was confused. Who then were his previous captors? Civil wars in that part of Africa were particularly complicated. He wanted to ask why they had rescued him, but decided the question might be premature. Perhaps he had exchanged one set of gaolers for another. The effects of the stress of the past few hours gradually overcame him and he slipped into a deep sleep.

He was awakened by a strange sensation. Lying on the bench opposite the two men, he realized the plane was making a steep descent. Before he rolled onto the floor, four pairs of hands secured him. A few minutes later he felt the sensation of the plane reaching the ground with a noise that became a grinding, throbbing groan. To his amazement, instead of a crash that was going to rend the entire fuselage and himself included, the plane made a remarkably smooth continuation of its journey onto the ground. Richard had experienced many worse landings at O'Hare Airport.

"Where are we?" Richard asked. "Don't worry. You'll be safely conducted to the American Embassy. My captain made arrangements," said one of the men. The other man, as before, remained placidly silent. "Who is this captain?" Richard asked. "Of course, the pilot of this craft is, may I say, the best pilot in all of Ethiopia." "Probably in all of Africa," the man replied proudly. "But, I don't understand," Richard insisted. "Why should you go to all this trouble to help me? I must give him my thanks at least." "I am very sorry, sir. But we have strict instructions. He is a great and important leader of our movement and must not be revealed to any of the authorities; but..." and then he groped beneath the seat, "...he asked that you have this; BUT...and he is very firm...DO NOT open until you are safely out of Ethiopia." The man then handed Richard a box tied together with string.

A black Peugeot was parked a few yards from the plane and he was hurriedly pushed into the back seat. The sun was beginning to rise. Richard stared from the back window and

115

thought he saw the dim figure in the cockpit waving.

What an experience this is, he thought. Then silently he offered up a prayer of thanksgiving for his deliverance.

He fingered the wrappings of the box in his lap and felt a strange urge to open it, but remembered the promise he had made. Doubts soon began to pervade his mind, What if it's contraband or drugs or whatever...What if they are using me as a courier? Despite his fears, Richard placed the box in the small bag which one of the men had given him. He glanced down at the snake boots two sizes too big that had also been lent to him and smiled.

Later that night, sitting in the hotel room, he tried to piece together the events of the past few days. By some series of miracles Richard had been secreted into the U.S. Embassy. It took some organization and some arguments to finally get him identity papers. After several phone calls to Geneva, he was given a money advance by the WHO and some kind of clothes.

Once again, he found himself at the luxurious Hilton International Hotel. It produced a strange deja vu. Perhaps it was the same room he had slept in fifteen years ago. But, on the other hand, most hotel rooms looked alike.

Why did those men, particularly the pilot, who never even showed his face to receive my gratitude, save me? he asked himself again and again and paced up and down the room. Then he remembered the box. Before he could stop himself he hurriedly pulled at the string and opened the lid and gasped. There was a pair of light, almost yellow-colored shoes with characteristic stitching on the front: his own shoes that had been stolen!

At the time Richard had cursed himself for wearing them

on this particualr trip. He couldn't explain why he had done that. He only wore them after all, on special occasions. He lifted them lovingly from the box and caressed the leather, weeping silently. A piece of paper fell to the ground. He picked it up and read, "My dear sir, I am sure it is you. I never forget a pair of shoes. As you will see, I have cleaned them again, but not as well as before. I was more professional then. Once again you can get them cleaned in a worthier fashion. By the way, as you will now realize, I have fulfilled my ambition. Not exactly an airline, but a good pilot, I hope you agree. Perhaps in better times we will meet again face to face. Meanwhile, your friend, the Shoeshine Boy of Addis Ababa."

PART 3

"Grampa, why do you have those shoes on the mantelpiece?" The young boy pointed to a glass case containing a pair of light, almost yellow-colored shoes that had obviously seen better days, but were far from worn out.

Richard leaned on his walking stick and then transferred his weight to his left arm, which rested on the fireplace. He pointed his stick gently and lovingly at the glass case. "Those are very special and precious shoes that I've had for many years. Do you know once they actually saved my life?"

The Baby-sitter

"This is Victoria, she will look after the children this evening while I am visiting my sick mother." Richard looked at the young African girl who he guessed was about sixteen years old. She was dressed in the typical long flowing dress of the local Baganda people. Although she was shorter than Richard, the slim features and the dress gave the illusion of being much taller.

Richard's friend, Bill Roberts and his wife were initially a little put out by the sudden announcement that the regular guardian of their children had decided to provide a substitute. It was too late to protest and no point in getting angry. They were already late for dinner and were meeting with several other friends at one of the few restaurants in the town Entebbe which was only 22 miles down the road from Kampala.

The dinner party was very successful indeed and everyone enjoyed themselves so much that time seemed to fly. This would not normally have been a problem, but when they returned to Roberts' house it became very clear that someone would have to take Victoria home. Richard immediately volunteered. "Where do you live?" he asked.

118

She replied simply, "Wandegeya." There was stunned silence as Richard and Roberts stared at each other in amazement.

Wandegeya although not far from the University campus where they were located was notorious. No white man ever ventured into this zone as far as Richard could remember. Even the African Police avoided the place. The area was a small tree filled valley between the main University campus and the main street of Kampala and only a dirt track lead from the main road into the densely wooded region. The only inhabitants were regarded as a race of criminals and bandits. Fruit bats occupied the high branches of the trees and at sunset every evening flew in large numbers to unknown destinations for the night.

Roberts broke the silence, "I had better come with you Richard. It would be more prudent if there were two of us". Richard nodded. He was greatly relieved to know that on this potentially hazardous journey he would not be alone.

It only took a few minutes to drive from Roberts' house to the area closest to Wandegeya. At this point they stopped the car and parked off the road under one of the nearest trees. Roberts was about to bid Victoria good night when she said simply, "please take me to the village, I'm afraid of walking in the dark". Richard was speechless. Roberts said something which sounded like "hell and I'm not sure what to do in the dark either". Having come this far they prepared themselves for the inevitable conclusion of their task and followed the girl along the narrow pathway that rapidly disappeared into the darkness of the trees. The city of Kampala and the University campus seemed to be hundreds of miles away in another world.

119

The young girl walked rapidly with a light step with no apparent cares in the world. Richard and Roberts had great difficulty keeping up with her and there were times when she would disappear around the end of the narrow track that lead deeper and deeper into the valley of the trees.

At one point she was so far ahead that when they reached a fork in the trail they were forced to stop. "Now which way do we go?" Roberts said testily. Richard shrugged and proceeded along the right path. "We have a 50-50 chance of being right" he said over his shoulder. Roberts reluctantly followed.

The path took a sharp bend around the base of a large tree and quite suddenly there was a mud hut with a straw roof and a small fire adjacent to the path around which three men were smoking their pipes. They looked up abruptly; their eyes wide with amazement as Richard and Roberts rushed past them and jumped over a small stream which appeared to function as a drainage ditch.

"Jambo" Richard briefly addressed the startled men. One of the men replied in a dialect Richard did not understand but thought it might be Luganda. The important language in that part of Uganda. "What is he saying?" Richard said as he and Roberts proceeded down the pathway. "Roughly translated he said that Victoria is quite a girl, she's even got two white men following her home".

They suddenly entered a clearing in which there were numerous mud huts arranged in a haphazard fashion. The only illumination came from a few oil lamps and a moderate sized fire in the center of the clearing.

There was Victoria standing in front of one of the huts smiling and waving to them. "Thank you very much, good night." She said then disappeared into the hut. "Now what the heck do we do?" Roberts said. "Well, I suppose we make our way home," Richard replied "that is of course if we can remember the way back". Roberts looked at Richards and his shoulders sagged. "Its not only a question of finding the way back through the woods, but will the car be there?"

The young men proceeded to re-trace their way back along the path. When they reached the hut where they had encountered the three men, no one was there. In fact they had not seen a single man since that encounter, not even in the main village. This was very disconcerting to Richard but he did not share his discomfort with Roberts who appeared to have enough of his own.

"This must be the way. Look I think I can see the road ahead" Roberts said. Richard was about to say "where is the" when both of them saw the green Mercedes under the tree exactly where they had left it. "I hope the damn wheels are still on it." Roberts said. "Well I can see the right side wheels from here" Richard said with a note of optimism rising in this voice.

Both of them started to walk briskly which developed into a run until they were brought to an abrupt halt by the appearance of several men emerging from the trees on both sides and one standing between them and the car.

"Oh hell! I knew things would go wrong. Try and act calmly please" Roberts said. Richard had no idea of what to say or do and stood with sweat pouring down the back of his neck.

As the men closed in around him, a tall individual who had been leaning on the car walked slowly towards them.

121

Before Richard and Roberts could think of anything to say the man smiled, his white teeth shining in the darkness. "Do not be afraid gentlemen. You are among us as friends" he said in a very clipped, but good English. It was difficult to tell exactly how he was dressed in the dim lights from the nearby road lights but both he and his colleagues wore very dark clothes which made them seem even more mysterious and frightening. "It was very brave and good of you to bring home our little girl, Victoria."

Richard strained his eyes to see to see the features of this man who appeared even taller as they approached but it was impossible. Your car has been well guarded and nothing is missing. Even the police would not dare to leave their vehicles in this spot. Everywhere you go in Uganda some of our people will be watching you and protecting you. Please now go." with that they all disappeared into the trees leaving Richard and Roberts standing by the car bewildered. "Lets get out of here and back home before someone changes their mind" Roberts said as he jumped into the drivers seat. They drove back onto the road and oblivious to any speed limit, reached home in record time.

Richard thought about the experience of entering that forbidden zone so close to the heart of the city and in normal circumstances would have gladly boasted of his escapades to his colleagues in the pathology department at the hospital. Somehow the profoundness of the occasion prevented him and after a week or so was hidden away in the depths of his memory.

Late one afternoon working at his microscope he was disturbed by a knock on the door and before he was able to rise and answer it, his friend Roberts burst into the room large as life. "I know its terribly short notice, but I wondered if you would like to come to a cocktail party tonight on the University campus. These are old friends and we would love you to join us".

Richard had no particular plans that night and rarely ever refused an opportunity to socialize. The party was at a house that was only a short distance from where Richard lived and he decided to walk. Although Kampala is on the equator, at 4000 feet above sea level the evenings are cool and very pleasant. By the time he reached the house it was obvious that the party was in full swing. He elbowed his way throughout several groups of people who had spilled out on to the lawn and the grounds outside the house. Richard was already enjoying his first gin and tonic before Roberts and his wife made their way towards him. "I'm so glad you were able to make it Richard" Roberts said. Richard exchanged some pleasantries with both Roberts and his wife and eventually was introduced to the hosts of the party who were an elderly couple from the USA working in the Geography Department. It was then that Richard met the Motani brothers.

The younger Motani did most of the talking. His accent was so impeccably English that if Richard had not seen the brown color of his skin he would have taken him for an Oxfordian. He was almost the same height as Richard and was very animated. What was not in keeping with his accent was the use of hands to illustrate the points he was making. Richard liked him immediately and they developed a detailed conversation about all sorts of subjects. The older Motani who was several inches taller than Richard and his younger brother stood passively smiling. In fact it was only was only at the end of the evening when Richard was making his attempt to leave the party that the older Motani spoke. "My brother and I would be delighted and honored if you would join us at our home in Kampala for drinks shall we say next week. We will send a note to you in the Pathology Department to confirm. This has been a great pleasure. Good night."

Richard walked home in the moonlight, pleased with himself and feeling good about having made new friends. He was particularly looking forward to meeting the Motani brothers again.

"What do you mean you're going up country with the Motani brothers?" Richard said as he tried without success to extricate a jacaranda blossom from his glass of beer. "Those Ismailis would sell you for a few shillings you idiot". There you go again with your damn racism and intolerance" Richard said angrily. "So you Welshman know more about bloody East Africa than a man who has been here most of his life I suppose," Roberts replied, finally throwing most of the remaining beer on the ground as he grasped the sodden jacaranda blossom.

Before Richard could reply, Roberts signaled to the waiter "Bring us two more Nile Laagers". Richard sat looking into his beer oblivious of the other occupants of the garden of the Speke Hotel".

He normally would have enjoyed his evening sitting under the great jacaranda tree that dominated the area between the hotel lobby and the main street of Kampala. He could not easily shake off years of Socialist upbringing in the small coal mining village in South Wales where he was born. Even during his medical student days and hospital residency training he would usually have defended a left-wing opinion rather than the conservative right winged environment in which he found himself. In the seven or eight months that he had lived in Uganda he had continuously found himself at odds with his previous ideas. The social structure of East Africa was very confusing. Three races and three religions mingled in a somewhat unsteady and unpredictable manner. The rival sounds of church bells from the cathedrals on two opposite hills and calls to the faithful from the minaret of the Mosques and the constant sound of Indian music from shops and Indian restaurants seem to epitomize the atmosphere.

Richard had tried very hard to socialize with the different racial representatives of the country. There was no problem in the course of the working day at the hospital, medical school or in the shops and banks in town. When it came to private social intercourse he felt frustrated. He had often invited African colleagues to his house, but always got excuses and he was never invited to theirs. It was therefore particularly important to him that he appeared to have made friends of the Motani brothers who had broken through the barriers.

In contrast, Bill Roberts was an outspoken direct Englishman who had spent most of his life in various countries of East Africa. He was the registrar of the University and had befriended Richard from the first day of his arrival. At first Richard found his startling, negative opinions regarding East African Indians or even visiting Americans disturbing. But after a few weeks he began to realize that this bluff large Englishman who seemed to be the symbol of the old colonial powers was in fact a more tolerant man than he had been in his first impression. Although his viewpoint on many subjects particular to race and behavior of different races was narrow it was at least consistent and to Richard's surprise the Africans and East African Indians seemed to have great respect for him. In the few months that they had known each other an unspoken agreement developed regarding their differences of opinions and life experiences. This particular evening however those differences exploded verbally and rather violently.

"I'm concerned about your safety" Roberts said. "Its got nothing to do with what you perceive as my prejudices. There is some evidence, circumstantial granted, that those Motani brothers have been involved in activities that lead to one of the English Expatriots here to be imprisoned and believe me you don't want to see inside a Uganda jail."

"Bill, I appreciate your concern" Richard said "but I'm only accepting a lift as far as West Nile District. You know my research interests in pigment spots on the feet and malignancy, well West Nile is an important area for me".

"But why go with the Motani brothers?" Roberts said. The tone of his voice rinsing with his anger.

"There is no one else free to go this weekend. Your busy so it seems is everyone else and the profesor won't let me travel such distances on my own". Richard said with a note of exasperation in his voice "so lets leave it now, enjoy our beer jacaranda flowers and all".

Richard barely reached his house and was about to sit down to his usual lonely dinner when Sam, his house boy, announced a visitor. Roberts strode into the room "I'm coming with you".

"What do you mean?" Richard said leaning back in his chair. "I thought you were busy."

"That has changed" Roberts interrupted him "Janice understands and is willing for me to travel with you."

"But I've already agreed to drive Motani Jr." Richard said.

"That is okay. I'd come with you in his car, as a matter of fact, Janice needs mine this weekend anyway" Roberts said.

Richard sighed. He felt a sense of relief that his good friend would be accompanying him on this journey despite the misgivings of the prospect of Roberts vs. Motani at close quarters for several days.

Roberts insisted on sitting in the front passenger seat having made formal introduction to young Motani. Richard had the luxury of the entire back seat and so stretched out to enjoy being driven up country. On his past Safaris he had been the driver and on those dirt roads only allowed himself the occasional glance left and right. On this beautiful morning just after the sun had risen he was able to look about as the car sped along the dirt road leaving a great cloud of red dust behind.

Every now and again throughout the gap in the banana plantations he could see a small cluster of round huts with small children playing on the hard baked ground outside their primitive homes.

Whenever the people waived and smiled Richard returned their gestures. His two companions however either stared ahead or engaged in a stilted conversation about the future of Uganda.

It was indeed the pessimistic view of the future of this country that appeared to be the most common ground between Roberts and Motani. They both had a fear of General Idi Amin taking over the country.

As the conversation became more heated Richard dozed off. He was startled back into consciousness by the sound of the horn and the screeching of the breaks, followed by considerable acceleration. He sat up and looked out of the back window into a cloud of red dust with feathers flying in all directions and people screaming and shaking their fists at the retreating car. "What the hell was all that about?" Richard said.

"I'm afraid that there is one chicken less in that small town" Motani said smiling.

"But -- --" Richard was about to say.

"I told you a hundred times that you never stop for any kind of accident on these roads" Roberts said.

"He's right my friend" Motani added. "It does not seem to matter to these people whether it is a chicken or goat or even a child. If we had stopped there is strong possibility we may have been beaten to death before the police can arrive."

Richard slumped back into his seat "I don't think I'll ever understand this country completely" he said to himself.

Despite the accident, it was a very pleasant change to be driven by a skilled driver in a fast car. By late afternoon, they were approaching the ferry across the Nile. Long lines of people, with the characteristic features of the Sudanic tribes of the northwest, were walking up the road from the river. The women were carrying huge burdens, effortlessly balanced on their hands. The men, of course, carried nothing. They were taller and much darker skinned than the Bantu people seen around Kampala.

The river was much wider and more placid than the turbulent, rock strewn water that burst from Lake Victoria. Its banks began to show the papyrus groves which would be so profuse further north where the great river enters the Sudan on the Sudanese border. The river's gentleness was misleading as the slow course of the ferry soon attested. The three of them stood leaning on the car and watching as the boat shuddered its way across the current.

Richard could not take his eyes off his fellow passengers. Several times he found himself staring at their feet, already anticipating pigment patterns, and the final chapters of his thesis.

Had the grimacing glances of Motani, not prevailed, he might have started the study, then and there.

The road north followed the west bank of the Nile through villages and towards the papyrus swamps which skirted the river's edge. Every few miles clusters of women and children could be seen bathing and washing their clothes. They were cheerful, exuberant people, who laughed and sang a great deal in the cool of the evening.

The town of Rhino Camp was not very impressive. The only substantial building was the jinnery. Motani left Richard and Roberts at the car and entered the front door of the building.

"This is a one horse town." Roberts remarked casually as he stretched himself.

"More like a half horse town, if you ask me." Richard

129

commented as he smiled at his surroundings.

Motani soon joined them accompanied by one of his countrymen, the manager of the jinnery, who seemed very pleased to greet them all officially. The little round faced man, dressed in an off white shirt and an even less white shorts, was almost ecstatic at the prospect of hosting the company at his home which he insisted was very close by.

His bungalow was surprisingly large, but Richard and Robert never did find out how many it normally housed. In typical East African Indian fashion the females of the family were not introduced or even seen.

The African servants were sent into a flurry of activity. Beer was served only to the two white men. Since Ismailis do not drink alcohol. Before long, as they sat relaxing on the veranda overlooking the river, the unmistakable aroma of spicy food began to permeate through the house, and made them realize how hungry they were.

By the time the food was served, enough beer had been consumed to make them a little tipsy. A good curry must never be hurried in the preparation or in the eating. An enormous meal was laid for the four of them in a spacious dining room. There didn't appear to be any cutlery, but it soon became clear that the custom was to use the pieces of flat hard bread to shovel the food into the mouth.

Richard was tired after dinner, too tired to stay up, and left the two Asians jabbering in their own tongue. Robert had already gone to his room, convinced that the generosity of the East African Indians at times was staggering.

After breakfast, Motani simply told Richard that he could use the car to continue his journey to Arua and the return to Kampala. Motani it seemed had business to deal with there, which would require his presence for several days and his friend would drive him home later.

The journey back to Kampala was relatively uneventful at least until they were only within a few miles of the city. Roberts was much more his ebullient self. He even reluctantly admitted that perhaps he had been too harsh in his criticism of Motani "after all" Roberts said "he did lend us his car to return in".

"You know we have a saying in England that you never lend another man, however close a friend, your wife, your fountain pen or your car."

Richard smiled recognizing the well-known and very English quotation. "This Peugeot is a very expensive car and certainly a great improvement on my old Ford" Richard said.

Their pleasant and amicable conversation was abruptly ended by the appearance ahead of a road barrier with police and army personnel blocking the road. "Now what's happening?" Richard said.

"Now I want you to remain calm and stay quiet" Roberts said "I will do the talking. Is that clear?" Richard nodded and eased the car to a halt in front of the barrier. An officer in the uniform of the Uganda army walked across slowly and imperiously.

Before the police officer could explain, Roberts immediately spoke in his best and most dominant English accent "What appears to be the trouble officer? I am Mr. Roberts the registrar of the University in Kampala and my colleague is Dr. Jones an eminent pathologist at the medical school and Mulago Hospital". The aggressive approach obviously had it effects and Roberts immediately followed up before the officer could even open his mouth "and we have been engaged in medical research in the West Nile District and are returning to the medical school. We would appreciate if we could continue our journey as soon as possible. We are already late." The policeman seemed at first puzzled, then smiled, saluted and waived them on.

It was several minutes before Richard spoke "Do you always deal with authority in that incredible arrogant and aggressive way?" Roberts smiled, "One thing I've learned in the years I have spent in Africa is that they respect authority and are more likely to respond to someone who appears to have no doubts about intentions and as you see it works."

Richards sat back, closed his eyes and began to think of the differences between them. Bill Roberts was a confident arrogant Englishman who knew Africa so well, the very epitome of the colonial administrator. Whereas Richard with his background in a coal mining village in South Wales and famous medical school in London, didn't quite know where he belonged. It was amazing to him that the two of them had struck up such a strong friendship.

Richard took Roberts to his home and declined the offer of a drink and returned to his own house. He parked the Peugeot next to his old Ford with the intentions of returning it to Motani the following day.

Theft was an integral part of life in East Africa. All newcomers were dutifully warned of various ways in which they could be relieved of their possessions. Richard had so far been very fortunate. That morning he awoke to a bewildering variety of sounds. His houseboy, Sam and his entire family and the garden boys were weeping and wailing as if at a funeral. Richard struggled into his dressing gown and followed an almost incoherent weeping young girl, one of Sam's numerous family. There was his Ford, propped up on logs of wood all four wheels missing. As if that wasn't bad enough, he suddenly became aware of the fact that Motani's Peugeot was nowhere to be seen.

His staff and families continued their cacophony. He felt like hitting them not because of their lack of diligence in protecting his possession, but their persistent remorse added to his black humor.

Richard sent his garden boy to one of the neighbors to ask for help. None of the junior faculty and most of the senior faculty had telephones in Uganda in those days.

While he was drinking his extra non-scheduled coffee, his house boy Sam ushered in two uniformed policeman.

"You must come with me to police station" the taller policeman said without any indication of emotion.

"Why what appears to be the problem?" Richard said nervously.

"You'll be notified of the reason sir when you accompany us" the policeman said.

Richard had never driven in a police car before and he felt very uncomfortable in the way they drove down the familiar road from the University campus past the wooded area of the Wandegeya to the police station.

To his horror he was ushered into a small room with bars on the windows and left alone for what seemed like ages. He paced up and down the small room like a caged animal. He could not see out since the only window was high up and barely letting in the light of day. Finally the door burst open and one of the policemen that had driven him to the police station entered accompanied by a more senior officer.

"You are Dr. Richard Jones I believe" the senior office asked.

Before Richard could answer the man continued "you drove a Peugeot 404 from Rhino Camp to Kampala yesterday?"

"Well yes I actually did that although it's not my car."

"And where is that car now Dr. Jones?" the senior policeman said staring down at him. "I've no idea" Richard said, "It was stolen during the night".

The tall senior policeman looked a little puzzled.

"We have reason to believe that the car was used to smuggle certain items into Kampala and therefore you must remain in custody here until we look into this first".

Richard was rarely at a loss for words, but his throat seemed to seize up on him and the dryness of his pallet made it impossible for him to respond. He was ushered along a narrow corridor and then down several flights of stairs into the basement of the police station and the door was thrown open and he was pushed into the most horrible room that he had ever encountered or could have imagined in his life.

He realized he was in some kind of cell blocks which consisted of a series of cubicals with a sloping floor extending down into a central trough or drain and both the appearance and the smell was like a primitive lavatory.

It was obvious that the occupants of these small bare cubicals had their excrement washed into the central trough down into the drainage system.

Richard felt a strong wave of nausea which almost

overcame him. It was all he could do to prevent himself from vomiting. The thought of being locked in this horrible place made him shake with fear.

One of the policemen stepped over the central drain and opened one of the cubicals and motioned Richard to enter. The area was approximately 6 foot by 6 foot with bare walls and the large metal door extending to within a few inches of the ground. There was no furniture and smell was appalling.

The worst sensation however was when the door was slammed shut and bolts secured. There was now an added sense of claustrophobia to his other fears and discomforts. Tears screamed down his face and he sat in one of the corners, his knees hunched up to his chest.

Throughout his tears he began to pray earnestly that somehow God would break into this terrible nightmare and bring him back to reality.

Richard had no idea how long he sat crouched in that cell oblivious to the noise and activities of the other inmates on either side of him or across the drainage channel. A mental numbness had overcome him and mercifully produced a form of temporary amnesia. He was suddenly shaken out of his torporous state by the sound of the door to his cell being opened. He stared in horror wondering what was install for him next.

In the dim light was his friend Roberts. "Richard my dear fellow" Roberts said. Uncharacteristically showing considerable emotion, "Lets get the hell out of this wretched place". He turned to the two policemen "there will be the devil to pay for this outrage I assure you. Arresting an innocent man and throwing him in here

135

without any evidence, Judge Justice Jones has already expressed his great anger over this."

Richard glanced at the frightened looking policeman and the image flashed through his mind of the corpulent Welsh Judge, Justice Jones, who was one of the most delightful, social characters but in the courtroom and in the justice system a very strong and powerful character.

Richard remembered the delightful evenings he spent at the judges house standing around piano singing Welsh songs, but the look on the policeman's face reminded him of how recently that jovial old Welshman had openly challenged the government of Uganda including the up and coming tyrant - Armin.

Roberts lifted Richard to his feet and pushed away one of the policemen who attempted to assist them.

"It's a damned good thing I was with you on that trip and Justice Jones is easily available"

Richard curled up in the back of Roberts' car and as they drove towards the University campus and passed the wooded area of Wandegeya, Richard gazed distractedly out of the window and for just a second thought he saw someone waving to him.

Back at Roberts' house and after a couple of stiff gin and tonics he began to come around. "You know Richard this is a very strange set of circumstances. I've warned you about the Motani brothers. Didn't I?"

"I'm not sure I understand you" Richard said as he sat up from his relaxed position in a large armchair. "What's this all got to do with Motani?"

"Now that is the easiest part to explain" Roberts said as he lit his pipe.

"The police informed us that they had been given a tip that the Peugeot of Motani contained some packages which were smuggled gems and other items which the Motani brothers use to get currency out of Uganda. If that car had not been stolen you would really have been in trouble. The mystery is the car was found intact on one of the side streets in Kampala and the police searched it thoroughly indeed and found no evidence to incriminate you."

Richard sat there amazed and unable to comment. "You know as well as I do that if anyone loses a car in Uganda they are lucky to see it and if you ever do it will be completely stripped down to the chassis" Roberts said. "It sounds crazy but it would seem that some actually did you a great favor by stealing that car and removing the evidence".

At this point Richard rose to his feet, put his drink down on the side table and paced up and down the room. "Well what about the Motanis? What explanation do they have for us?"

"They have already fled the country boy" Roberts said, the smile breaking out all over his face. Of course, once they discover the loss of evidence they will probably return and start again.

Later that night as Richard was preparing for bed his house boy, Sam, came into the room and handed hin a scrap of paper. "What is this all about?" Richard said. It was pinned to the kitchen door" Sam said abruptly.

Richard stared at the wrinkled scrap of dirty paper and the barely legible script said "for the sake of Victoria".

He walked out onto the back porch staring up into the

star filled night. "God certainly moves in mysterious ways, but through a baby-sitter!"

MARTIN GWENT LEWIS

IN PURSUIT

OF THE NILE PERCH

PART I
First Encounter

*F*ishing had always been one of Richard Jones' great passions. He really was more fond of this particular sport than any other. In fact, it was his only real sporting activity. He hated watching team games, even more than he hated participating in them. But to go off, with a rod and line, and stalk anything that swam in any kind of water, was to him, the greatest of activities outside of his work.

By the time he reached East Africa his greatest catch was a two pound striped perch, which he caught one day in a pond half way up the mountain near his home in South Wales. Uganda was to provide him fishing opportunities beyond his wildest dreams.

Since the really good fishing spots in Uganda required considerable travelling, he made himself available for a variety of medical safaris, often with minimal excuse.

139

Some of his colleagues felt a little resentful that he was allowed to do this so often. The professor reasoned that Jones had a great ability to act diplomatically and to solve problems in many of the up country hospital laboratories such as they were. Richard also had another unlikely project; at least it seemed so to others in the department of pathology. He was plotting pigment patterns on the soles of the feet of the Africans and relating them to a particular form of malignant melanoma. This of course, required him to visit every single tribal area in the country and survey the population. This became a very handy way of being able to explore the various waterways of the country with his fishing equipment always in the back of the car.

Richard's first encounter with the great fish of East Africa, the Nile perch, was the result of his tendencies to make a wide variety of friends. On this particular occasion he had been getting his car serviced in a small mechanic shop down in the heart of Kampala. The son of the owner, who did most of the work on the car, was a young Mahrahta, one of the warrior race of India, who was even shorter in stature than Richard, but clearly a very wild character in many respects.

Considering there was very little deep social intercourse between the races in East Africa, it was not very often that white men were ever invited to either African or Indian homes. That was not the case with Richard Jones. He soon found himself invited to the home of his car serviceman, who, it turned out, had been educated in England.

Richard's first visit to the home of his friend was, to

some extent, an embarrassment to the young Indian, who although educated in the western world and regarding himself as a sophisticated man, was forced to live in his father's home by the traditions of his people. He tried to apologize to Richard in advance.

It was a strange evening. The men folk sitting around the perimeter of the room, the center of which was empty, except for a large carpet. From time to time he would hear giggling from the next room and see eyes peering through the curtains. These, it turned out were the female members of his friend's family. It was considered unsuitable for them to be seen by a male visitor. The father explained that he would not insult his guest by introducing him to the female members of his family. Yet, the old man had no compunction about introducing an old African servant, as if he was a more revered member of the family, than his own wife and daughters. Despite these differences in tradition, Richard struck up a firm friendship with the young Indian mechanic, and was, a few weeks later, invited to go on a fishing trip on the Nile.

As promised, the car mechanic, accompanied by two of his young male relatives, arrived at Richard's house at the crack of dawn. He had been instructed only to bring his clothes and a hat and that all else would be provided. That was certainly the case. The East African Indians have often been accused of greed, avarice and cheating, but as Richard discovered, when they befriend someone, they are generous beyond belief.

They drove through the empty streets of Kampala onto the main road east toward Jinja. It wound through the small towns still mostly asleep in the early cool of the beginning

141

of another African day. After an hour on the main road, they turned off and headed north through much less inhabited bush and scrub land with fewer and fewer towns. The road remained better surfaced than the main road, largely since it was newer, and had been used less frequently. After nearly another hour, they turned abruptly onto a small track that seemed to run haphazardly through the trees.

This was Richard's first experience on an Ugandan dirt road and he felt convinced at the time that the driver must have been crazy or had made a big error. It did not seem possible that this was meant to be driven over. The red dust, known throughout East Africa as murrum, seemed to be everywhere, and covered him down to his underwear.

After what seemed an age, but was only about half an hour, they suddenly came around a sharp bend in the road and saw below them the great river that has captured the imagination of so many since recorded time, the Nile. This cradle of one of the world's greatest civilizations even in its early stages was already a great vibrant powerful stretch of blue, flecked with white foam where fast currents broke over enormous rocks. The river and its shallow small valley were flanked on all sides by dense green undergrowth and papyrus beds. It seemed from the elevation, in which the car stood that they had no access to the banks of the river. However, after a short winding descent, the road broadened into a clearing in which there was a small collection of huts and a landing jetty projecting into the stream. A ferryboat of ancient design was making its way painstakingly from the opposite banks fighting the obviously powerful current. The river at this point was approximately fifty miles from

142

its source in Lake Victoria and, despite its width was still very much a mountain stream. While the Indians parked the car and made arrangements with the locals to guard it for the day, Richard stared about in wonderment and delight. The river seemed even wider than it had appeared from a distance.

They finally boarded the ferry, accompanied by a great assortment of African men, women and children, with goats, chickens, all sorts of bundles, and the inevitable bicycles. The ferry could carry about twenty people and their belongings, and it was full. Richard noticed the shy and varied glances of the women and children. Most of them were friendly to white men, as was most frequently the case in Uganda in those days. Their attitude, to the three Indians however, was not so warm and much more guarded. The Indians regarded them in the same way.

Uganda had been a protectorate of the British Crown for a number of years and no white man had been allowed to own land, so that the relatively few people of his race had served the Africans as leaders, engineers, missionaries and doctors. No real anti-white feelings had ever developed there as it had in other parts of Africa.

The relationship with the Asians, as they called all people of non-white and black origin, was somewhat less attractive. These transplants from India had been used by the colonial powers at the turn of the century to build the Uganda railway from Mombassa on the coast to Kampala. They settled and thrived and their descendants became the shopkeepers, traders, and eventually the businessmen of Kenya, Uganda and Tanganyika.

The Africans could not compete with these aggressive

and often ruthless people, who were prepared to work much harder and live almost anywhere, under almost any circumstances. When the white man left, the Asians stayed, clinging tenaciously to what they owned. Even the smallest town of any description in Uganda had an Indian duka, or garage, or combination of both. They could, and would sell almost anything. It was, however, their success as a group that proved to be their downfall. The "Jews of East Africa" was the name often given to them.

Richard's meditations were brought to a sudden halt when the ferry ground onto the opposite bank. He stepped onto the shores of Bunyoro, the Nile being the geographic border between the kingdom of Buganda and the next area to the east.

Although the entire country was theoretically under one government, the various kingdoms and tribal areas still retain certain autonomy and were distinctly separate in terms of language and custom.

The people with the typical Negroid features of the Bantus still looked much the same to him. The women still wore the long colorful dresses and the younger men a form of European dress. The older more dignified men wore a long white outfit, which looked like an old-fashioned-nightgown.

The group was greeted by a typical up-country East African Indian, who spoke to the others in Gujarati, at least as far as Richard could make out. A characteristic exchange occurred with gestures and pointing up and down the river in an excited chatter which he could not understand at all. He watched and tried to absorb it all while the Indians talked and the passengers from the ferry moved off into the adjacent green bush. He wondered where they could be going and what they would be doing.

Eventually, he realized the necessary preambles were over and they were herded toward a boat, which had been hired for the day. At first sight it looked reasonable enough, similar to the ferry but smaller and also made of metal. It was a glorified bathtub, with an outboard motor and a metal part roof to shield them from the sun. They loaded their pots and other boxes containing enough curry and beer to feed a small army. The fishing gear was loaded on and two Africans became the crew.

These locals spoke virtually no English, but certainly knew the river, and turned out to be quite expert at locating the fish. The six men pushed off into the current and soon were rapidly proceeding downstream. Richard sat back beneath the metal canopy and felt the warmth of the morning sun, and watched the papyrus on the banks, the fish eagles, and the ever-changing character of that amazing river. Life on the adjacent bank changed as dense papyrus gave way to open clearing with women from the local villages washing clothes in the water, their smiling children waving greetings. At times the experienced Africans at the rear of the boat guided them effortlessly between enormous rocks that danced the water in all directions. After an hour or so he was suddenly aware of the river widening into a bend that seemed to become a small lake. At this point, with great activity, the fishing lines were placed, and the boat slowed to change direction across the current. They gave him a fishing rod and he sat watching the tip bobbing gently with the action of the current. This change of pace soon settled into mesmerizing, slow, up and down rhythm, which caused him to doze quietly. Suddenly, he was jerked violently out of his daydreams by a searing pain in his right hand, as the line was torn off the screaming reel. He leapt to his feet as a great weight dragged him to the side of the boat. He quickly regained his control, checked the flow of line, and leaned back on the rod, as the excited members of his crew and his friends danced about with joy.

"What the hell is this?" Richard cried out, "Have I hooked the bottom or a crocodile or something?"

"No, a Nile perch," shouted his friend, the mechanic.

"A what?" Richard replied.

The biggest perch he had ever seen was barely more than two pounds in weight—this thing, whatever it was, seemed capable of dragging him overboard. At that point, the line curved towards the surface of the water, and about thirty yards from the boat an enormous fish jumped into the air. He nearly dropped the rod in utter surprise, but with much help from the others, regained control, and proceeded to play the fish. The next fifteen minutes or so were a combination of intense excitement, elation, and fear—that dreadful fear all fishermen experience when playing a really good fish and realizing that at any moment they might lose it. Several times he thought it had broken loose, and a depressing feeling came over him only to be rapidly dispelled by a mighty rush of the great fish. He was constantly encouraged by the others who gathered about shouting advice, whilst the Indian mechanic quietly kept close and urged him not to panic. Eventually the fish began to tire. So did Richard, but the adrenaline surging through his own blood kept him determined not to give in. For part of an hour he was "The Old Man and The Sea" and he knew how Hemingway must have felt.

Finally the fish rolled over close to the boat and one of the Africans plunged a great hooked gaff into the side of the gill. It took them all to lift the giant perch into the boat. Like excited children everyone clapped and cheered and shouted congratulations. Richard felt so flushed with success he was speechless and stood there smiling like a contented fool.

This fish was beautiful; a great silver shape with amber colored eyes. As he discovered later, it weighed seventy-five pounds.

This was the signal to break out the beer and everyone, including the African boatmen, drank a toast. Richard sat there staring with utter delight at the finest fish ever. It produced a feeling of such goodwill he genuinely wished that all of them would catch one before the hour was out. He did not care then if he caught another one. This was enough to satisfy him for all those luckless fishing trips of the past. What a wonderful country and world, he thought, this is the life!

The rest of the day produced three other Nile perch, but smaller. Richard had the catch of the day, which produced no sense of envy, whatsoever, amongst his new friends. They finally chugged their way slowly back upstream, and landed again near the ferry. Africans appeared from out of nowhere to watch whilst the fish were weighed. One of the smaller fish was given to the grateful African boatmen, and the little company, tired but contented, took the ferry back to the west bank of the Nile.

As they drove back to Kampala through the rapidly developing African dusk, Richard felt a sense of wholeness with himself. He could hardly wait to tell his story to his comrades in the department the next day, but before that he had to help Sam, his houseboy, fillet the great beast. He had enough Nile perch to feed most of his friends and neighbors.

PART II

*R*ichard's fishing escapades became so notorious that those visitors to the department were drawn towards him like lemmings.

One of these occasions was the result of a request from a group of very eminent visiting scientists of the National Institute of Health, and the National Cancer Institute in Washington, D.C.

Not only the four visitors and Richard, but also another carload of medical faculty members, traveled to the Nile that particular weekend.

They hired two boats for the day and decided that it was an ideal opportunity for a competition.

Richard decided to be clever and instead of downstream, went upstream, into a much more dangerous section where the river was turbulent. There were huge rocks, sometimes as big as townhouses strewn across the river like jagged islands.

He had been reading about Nile perch since his previous experience and began to think of himself as an expert. He reasoned that they lay between the shallows and

148

the deeps, where small fish come down over the rocks. The only problems were the difficulty in controlling the boat, and the caliber of the crew. Their fate was in the hands of a couple of Africans, one of who at the tiller had obviously been drinking waragi, very liberally.

At one point, Richard looked up, more out of instinct than anything else, and realized that the boat, instead of pointing upstream or downstream, was poised at an angle somewhere across the river. As a result, the strong current drove them downstream uncontrolled with the outboard motor almost useless.

The driver was asleep! Before Richard could shout to the other African or rush to the back of the boat, there was a resounding crash and everyone was pitched in all directions, some almost overboard.

They dropped their rods and looked around in great confusion. They were stuck on a large flat rock but still upright. One of the eminent professors from the National Cancer Institute, whose only previous experience had been on the Potomac in Washington, D.C., lost his nerve and became very excited.

The main problem was not only where they were stuck, but also they were approximately halfway across the river. There were no other boats in sight, and they were out of earshot and sight of the ferry or the Indian boathouse. The other African was not much help. A rapid council was called and Richard suggested that they try what he'd heard referred to as a 'sea anchor'. The truth of the matter was, he had really no idea what such a device was, or how to use it. But, luckily, the senior cancer researcher knew exactly what to do. Between them they attached the anchor to a

149

sturdy piece of rope and after several attempts, hooked it across a rock. With great effort, they gradually pulled themselves off the rock and back into the current.

The day wasn't a total disaster; they also managed to catch several perch, weighing between twenty to sixty pounds. It wasn't the most spectacular day in Richard's experiences, but the gentlemen from Washington were delighted. The group from Mulago Hospital, who had never been fishing before, was also proud of the fact that they won the competition. When the story reached the medical school the following day, one skeptical Canadian commented "Young Jones had the hierarchy of the N.C.I of the USA --poised on a rock -- ready to be crocodile food." There are some in Washington who might well have advanced their careers.

PART III

A special visitor came to the department of pathology and not just for a couple of weeks but for a year. He had been a professor in London for many years; retired, became a professor in the University of Ibadan in Nigeria for four years, then retired again and spent his second retirement year, as visiting professor, with the group in Kampala. He and his wife were in their seventies and had very active minds. His line of research, which led to some important discoveries, had a great influence on Richard's subsequent career.

At the morning coffee meeting, the professor announced in his bluff way, "Well, young Jones, I hear you fancy yourself as a bit of a fisherman."

"Well, I like to fish, sir." Richard replied.

"Sunday morning then you'll meet me and Isabelle, my wife, at exactly eight a.m. and we will drive to Jinja and fish in the source of the Nile. I've always fancied doing that and I think that this is a great opportunity to do so."

Eight a.m.! Richard's heart sank and he was about to protest, but the stern look from the older man silenced him.

The journey that Sunday morning, along the road to Jinja, with the professor at the wheel was a terrifying experience. Richard, glancing at the speedometer, wondered to himself how this man had survived into his seventies. He prayed that nothing; chicken, nor goat or child would venture into the road before they reached their destination.

The professor's wife was a charming lady. She was as unique and individual, as was her husband. In her youth she had practiced law and in recent years had been his laboratory technician. Richard remembered how, a few days before, he had gone to learn from the professor the art of growing cancer cells in small dishes. He found that the eminent man was away on a trip somewhere, something that he did quite frequently. Isabelle had been there as usual, busying herself around the lab, and when Richard suggested that she might give him instructions, fully realizing that it was she who did most the work anyway, her reply was so characteristic.

"Oh my dear boy, you must learn from the master. I am merely his handmaiden."

As the car almost flew through the small villages that dotted the route, Richard tried to imagine her as anyone's handmaiden. She seemed to sense his nervousness and concern and engaged him in light conversation.

"You know, Doctor Jones, that Rupert was a fighter pilot in the First World War and managed to survive for two and one half years, where the average life span was about six weeks." Richard wasn't particularly comforted by the thought, and wished he were, in fact, in an airplane rather than flying in a small Volkswagen.

The journey to the bridge at Jinja was made in record time.

"Well, where's this good spot to fish?" the professor asked.

"The best is on that promontory of rock that juts out over the edge of the falls there. But it's dangerous."

Richard was very hesitant since he had no intention of allowing the old man to expose himself to such danger.

"Well, if that's the best spot, that's where I'm going to fish." the professor announced, allowing no challenges.

Richard shrugged his shoulders and led him along the single narrow path to the promontory. It stood about one hundred feet above the unbelievable roaring water below. The object was to cast a fishing line across the stream at an angle, and draw it into the less turbulent water at the edge. The fish they were after were not as impressive as the Nile perch, but powerful, especially in that current. The main problem was how to get the fish out of the river and up the steep incline. So far, Richard had never heard of anyone catching a barbel and actually lifting it out of the water. The sport of hooking and playing them was the best part anyway, since nobody ate them.

Richard had underestimated his senior colleague. Having satisfied himself that he knew how to do the appropriate cast and retrieve, the professor made it very clear that since there was no room for two of them to stand on that very narrow rock, that Richard would have to go back and make pleasant talk with Isabelle. Reluctantly, Richard walked back down the steep and narrow pathway and found the old lady spreading a picnic lunch under the trees.

Despite her interesting stories, he found himself glancing nervously over his shoulder toward the rocky promontory. The professor's wife caught him and smiling, said, "Oh, don't worry about him, my boy, he's indestructible."

Richard was not particularly convinced and decided it was time to go and investigate. On reaching the top of the pathway, he suddenly became aware that no one was there. Realizing the only way down was the way he had already walked; a sudden panic seized him. He rushed to the edge of the rock and saw, to his amazement, the old man with the rod tucked under his arm. climbing up the side of the rock face, puffing and panting.

Richard assisted him over the final edge and the professor sat down, not looking particularly pleased.

"Oh, you'll be the death of me, my boy."

At this point, Richard could hold himself back no longer, and senior professor or not, felt obliged to raise his voice angrily.

"What do you mean, I'll be the death of you? I didn't tell you to go climbing down those rocks. That's dangerous down there."

"Well..." the professor interrupted, "my lure got stuck in the rock down there. It cost twenty-five shillings. I can't afford to lose tackle like that."

At this point, Richard realized that he had met his match.

He grew to love this old couple, who became his parents in science. They guided him to many of his subsequent scientific adventures. Still, he was very glad when that day was over.

A few days later at coffee, the sequel to the story was told. Apparently, people had seen the professor and Isabelle fishing at a very similar spot a little further down the river and the old man had hooked a huge barbel. It was estimated to be over twenty-five pounds, and in that current, it must have been a struggle. He brought it several times to the bank, but didn't quite have the strength to lift it on shore. The technician, who was telling the story, continued with great enthusiasm.

"...And we watched from the other bank and saw Mrs. Pulvertaft hoist her skirts up and walk into the water, up to her waist, and seize the fish, clasping it to her bosom, stride ashore again like Brunhilda coming out of the fires and the waves."

Everyone roared with laughter.

At this point, Professor Pulvertaft walked into the room and the laughter subsided a little.

"Well, what's the joke?"

Richard said, "I've just been hearing about your latest fishing trip and how Mrs. Pulvertaft brought the fish

154

ashore. That's quite a remarkable lady."

"Oh, I don't know," the professor replied, "damn it, man, what's the point of having a wife if they don't do something useful occasionally?"

PART IV

*R*ichard was driving home from the medical school early one evening, and chanced to see his old friend, Alan Reese, playing the inevitable game of tennis. He stopped and mentioned that he would be going off on safari the following weekend, with the department Land Rover, to do some research and visit hospitals as well as getting in a little fishing. Since he would be nearing Lake Albert, he thought it would be a great chance for some Nile perch.

"Well, the only snag is," said Reese, a haunted look on his face, "you know since that last trip, my wife is not very happy with the idea of me going off fishing, especially with you."

"Well, I think that's a bit much." Richard replied. "After all, whose idea was it to go sailing down the Nile in a rubber dinghy?"

Reese ignored the remark, "And not only that, but my brother from Britain is staying with us. But..." he stopped and thought for a moment.

Richard could see the deviousness creeping into his eyes. "...This of course would he a great opportunity to take my brother away on a trip. We don't have to mention anything about the circumstances, or what we plan to do. I do have some time off coming."

"Not only that," Richard offered, "but we could, for instance, camp. We have a large tent available, which would fit into the back of the Land Rover, which means that my university allowance for hotels could pay for the entire trip. You wouldn't be out of pocket at all."

This was the final persuasion. Alan vowed that come what man, he and his brother would be with him.

Early next morning, as the sun rose over the hills of Kampala, the three men, filled with a marvelous feeling of adventure, took the road Northwest toward a small township called Hoima, in the kingdom of Bunyoro, about 130 miles away.

The road was only paved from about 30 miles from the capital city and the dirt road was not particularly good.

Alan's younger brother was so different, that Richard wondered if they were really related at all, despite a certain facial similarity. Both of them were quite handsome young men, but the younger brother, Tom, was as quiet and thoughtful as the older one was extrovert and exuberant.

For most of the journey, Tom rarely said a word.

Reese found it necessary to lecture on the technique of using Ugandan highways. "On a dirt road, my boy, you drive right down the middle where the surface is the most even until you see an oncoming vehicle. If the oncoming vehicle is driven by a white man, you wait until both of you are reasonably close, then both veer a little to the side and press one hand against the windshield to prevent flying stones from shattering the glass."

156

He glanced to see if the two were listening.

"If the other car is driven by a Sikh, then pull well to the left, he'll probably hold his position and, only slightly, slow down. If on the other hand, it's a nun, get the hell out of the way, as far left as you can. She won't even notice you. But...' he paused and winked, '...if it's an Army truck, get into the ditch and hide."

They decided that Friday would be spent in travel and since no one would require them to be at the hospitals they were visiting on Saturday and Sunday, they had a glorious opportunity to fish Lake Albert two full days. They could drive Sunday evening to their next appointment.

They reached Butiaba, on Lake Albert, early in the evening, and just had time to erect the tent before one of those wonderful African sunsets drew them to the shore where they gazed across the mountains of the Congo, miles away. After the sun went down, a violent electrical storm broke over the far shoreline and hills, while the weather remained calm and clear on the Uganda side. The three of them sat there for nearly an hour, each lost in their own thoughts.

Richard, remembering the philosophy of one of his heroes,

Dr. Albert Schwietzer respected the other men's individuality and privacy and did not interrupt their solitude. To be able to sit with other human beings in silence, watching beauty, without feeling awkward, for Richard was the true sign of friendship.

The following day, they arose as early as possible and managed to hire a boat, with an African to assist them. They spent this beautiful day drifting in a great inland sea,

157

their lines trailing behind.

It was mid-afternoon before they had the slightest sign of fish. When the great perch struck, it was Richard, by great luck that was holding one of the rods. It literally nearly pulled his arms out of their sockets. The line screamed off the reel and the fish took at least 20 yards before he could dare check it. After the first feeling of tremendous resistance, the huge fish leapt clear out of the water into the air, shaking it's tail in fury. The sight was one Richard would always remember. The fish was even bigger than his first one.

The others shouted excitedly, as they maneuvered the boat for him. He played the great fish up and down until his arms were aching. He was not sitting in a specially constructed chair with the rod attached to a harness, and merely pumping the line, like a sportsman deep-sea fishing. Richard simply stood at the side of the boat, with the others hovering close to make sure he wasn't pulled into the water. He had to play the fish in the same way that he would have done a trout or a salmon.

Finally, they drew it to the side of the boat, and with the assistance of the African, dragged it aboard. It was a real beauty, with amber eyes, silvery sides, and huge dorsal fins, lying there defeated, but still alive. When it was weighed, much later, it was over 120 pounds.

"Oh, what a fish!" Richard exclaimed.

The African was even more delighted when the three white men gave him the fish to take home to feed his family.

"After all," Richard said, "how on earth are we going to carry this huge fish around for another three days without refrigeration?"

This kind of interaction between expatriates in East Africa, and the local African people, kept up an old long-time friendship, which did not exist in other parts of colonial Africa.

Subsequently they drove to the main town of the area, Masindi. It was decided that in honor of their great triumph, they would stay at the hotel on Richard's expense account and have the luxury of cold beer and a delicious meal. After dinner they sat on the verandah of the hotel, smoking their pipes. "I'm glad you brought your camera, Tom," Richard said, "Now I have proof that the biggest fish did not get away."